THE
CASE
OF THE
KIDNAPPED
ANGEL

THE CASE OF THE KIDNAPPED ANGEL

A MASAO MASUTO MYSTERY

E. V. CUNNINGHAM

DELACORTE PRESS/NEW YORK

Published by
Delacorte Press
1 Dag Hammarskjold Plaza
New York, N.Y. 10017

For Paul D. Reynolds

THE
CASE
OF THE
KIDNAPPED
ANGEL

The Kidnapped Angel

As a Buddhist policeman on the Beverly Hills police force, Detective Sergeant Masao Masuto abhorred superstition. For one thing, it went against his Zen training, for another, it defied common sense; so when a day began not only badly but improbably and continued in such manner, he refused to blame anything other than coincidence. The day was early in November, close to his birthday which marked him as a Scorpio; but his distaste for the nonsense called astrology—which pervaded Los Angeles—was as great as his distaste for any other superstition.

For all that, he found it quite extraordinary that he should be interrupted by a thief during his morning meditation. He had begun his meditation at six A.M., in the first faint gray light of dawn. His meditation room was a tiny sun porch at the rear of his Culver City cottage, where he lived with his wife, Kati, and his two children. Since the two children were of different sexes, there was no bedroom to spare. Masuto did not complain. Indeed, he was grateful for the nine-by-twelve sun porch, which was large enough, since it contained no furniture other than a meditation mat and pillow, and there he was, sitting on the pillow cross-legged in what is known as the lotus position, wrapped in his saffron-colored robe, when a sixteen-year-old Chicano boy forced open one of the windows, climbed through, and stood facing him.

For a long moment the Mexican boy stood motionless, staring at the nisei detective, who sat motionless, returning the stare. For Masuto, it was a double effrontery—first that a thief should invade a policeman's house, and second that he should be interrupted in his meditation. Then the boy, digesting the fact that Masuto was alive, turned to flee, and Masuto thrust out a leg and tripped him. Then, with the boy's arm in a hammerlock, Masuto said, "Get up and don't struggle, because if you do, your arm will be broken."

Kati, alarmed by the commotion, arrived at the meditation room in time to hear this, and her comment was, "I don't believe this. A little boy, and you threaten to break his arm?"

She was right. The Chicano boy was quite small. Masuto let go of his arm and led him from the room by the collar of his shirt. Masuto was slightly over six feet tall and, at this moment, somewhat ashamed of himself. The boy was skinny and shivering.

"I didn't do nothing. Let me go," the boy said.

"He's a thief," Masuto explained to Kati. Now Masuto's two children, Ana, age eight, Uraga, age ten, were also watching, standing in their nightclothes and regarding Masuto with what he could only interpret as accusatory stares.

"Why don't you let him go?" Kati asked.

"He's a thief. I'm a policeman."

"You're a cop?" the boy said. "My God, I got as much brains as a cockroach, breaking into a cop's house."

"What's your name?" Kati asked him.

"Pedro."

"And you're hungry. Did you have any breakfast?"

He shook his head.

"And that did it," Masuto explained to his partner an hour later in the homicide office of the Beverly Hills police force. "This kid breaks into my house, and Kati feeds him."

"You know what it is, Masuto. It's those consciousness-raising sessions she's been going to. Did you call the Culver City cops?"

"No."

"You let him go?"

"I have to live with my wife. Anyway, he swore up and down he'd never done it before and wouldn't do it again, and the only weapon he had on him was a screwdriver. If I turn him over to the cops, it's either a suspended sentence or juvenile. Either way, he gets a record and maybe worse."

Masuto's partner, Detective Sy Beckman, nodded. "Maybe you're right. But I hate these stupid kids. Amateurs. We can deal with the professionals, but the amateurs screw things up. I don't know—no more lines of professional pride. These days everything is amateur. Maybe this kidnapping too. It has the earmarks."

"What kidnapping?"

"Angel Barton was kidnapped, and the captain's car was stolen. The two ain't connected, except that Wainwright's sore as hell. That's a coincidence—your house broken into and Wainwright's car stolen. Do you suppose they're after the Beverly Hills cops?"

"When did that happen?"

"The car?"

"No, the kidnapping."

"Sometime last night. I just got here ten minutes ago, so I'm not filled in on the details. Wainwright threw these files at me to play shuffleboard with—they're all on people associated with Mike Barton, but from here what we got is strictly nothing."

"Where's the captain now?"

"In his office with a roomful of civilian brass. He called twice to ask where the hell you were."

At that moment the telephone on Masuto's desk rang. He picked it up and Wainwright's voice asked him where the hell he was.

"I'll be right in."

In the dozen steps between his office and Captain

Wainwright's—he was chief of detectives in the Beverly Hills police force—Masuto tried to remember and piece together what he knew about the Bartons. He knew at least a little and sometimes a great deal about most of the celebrities who lived in Beverly Hills, which is not to say that he knew many of them personally. What he knew of the Bartons had been gleaned from newspapers and from his wife, Kati, who was a much more enthusiastic movie fan than Masuto. Mike Barton was one of a half-dozen or so bankable stars, which meant that his name alone, associated with a film project, was enough to bring in the financing necessary to make the film. It was said that he had been paid a million and a half to star in his last film and that he was asking two million for his next. He was a tall, well-built man, with a craggy face, russet hair, and blue eyes, and given the right director, he could perform as an actor. Masuto tried to recall him on the screen, and while he felt he must have seen one of his films, he was not absolutely certain.

Concerning Barton's wife, Angel, his information had come totally from Kati, who read the gossip columns and pored over the picture magazines and was absolutely enchanted by both the name and the public image of Angel Barton.

The most intriguing thing about Angel Barton was that she had no traceable past, not even a real name available to the columnists on *The Hollywood Reporter* and *Daily Variety*. When questioned on this subject, she simply smiled her wonderful smile, and her husband, in reply to the same question, told reporters that since her name was Angel, she had obviously dropped from heaven. He himself had christened her Angel, and neither of them would discuss any prior existence. This was taken by the media as a publicity stunt, and while several enterprising reporters set out to discover who Angel actually was, none of them were successful. The secret was well kept.

And as Kati had put it to her husband, "She does look like an angel." More precisely, she looked like the romantically remembered Marilyn Monroe, with the same golden curls and wide blue eyes. She had a very faint, almost indiscernible foreign accent which no one could place and a way of making any man she spoke to feel that he was the most important member of the male world. She and Mike Barton had been married two years ago, but whether it was her first marriage or not Kati had never mentioned. The rest of what Kati had told him about Angel Barton was of no great consequence, nor could Masuto recall much of it as he entered Captain Wainwright's office.

The small office was crowded. Joe Smith, the city manager was there, along with Al Freeman, who was the mayor—an honorary, unpaid job—and three other men, introduced in turn as Frank Keller of the FBI, very young, very pompous; Jack McCarthy, Barton's lawyer; and Bill Ranier, Barton's business manager. McCarthy was in his late fifties, overweight, sure of himself, with a wide local reputation among film people; Ranier was middle forties, thin, nervous, impatient.

Wainwright wasted no time. "This is Masuto," he told Ranier and McCarthy. "I'll settle for him and his partner, but I can't have hands off. Once Barton informs the police, it's a police matter."

"I know, I know," said McCarthy. "I advised him. But you know damn well, Captain, that a smart kidnapper will not pick up the ransom if he suspects a trap."

"Jack," the mayor said soothingly, "if there's one thing we're all together on, it's that nothing must happen to Angel. But Barton can't handle this alone."

"He's not alone. He has Bill and me."

"Not enough," Wainwright said. "You know that as well as I do, Mr. McCarthy. I'll tell you what I'll do. I know Barton's convinced that his house is being watched and that maybe there's even an inside connection, and we got to respect the threat that his wife will be killed if he even speaks to the cops. There'll be no phone taps, and the feds will use our place here as their command post. Now Sergeant Masuto here is the best man we got. A hell of a lot of gardeners are Japanese or nisei. We'll fit Masuto up with a gardener's pickup and he'll change his clothes and drive out to Barton's place and go in through the back door the way a gardener would. Barton's an actor, so he can raise hell with Masuto for interrupting him today if anyone's listening and then he can find a way to talk to Masuto alone."

"I don't know whether Barton will buy that."

"He'll buy it," Freeman said. "I'll drive out first and talk him into it. But when it comes to the drop he wants to be alone, absolutely alone."

"Let him work that out with Masuto," the city manager said. "Barton has the last word, but when there's a crime in our city limits and we're informed, we have an obligation to pursue it."

"I'll arrange for the car," Wainwright told them. "Nothing's going to happen until the banks open. I'd appreciate it if one of you filled Sergeant Masuto in. Then he can go home and change clothes, and still get to Barton's soon after nine."

"I'll go there now," Freeman said, and then asked McCarthy, "are you worried about carrying the money, Jack? I can meet you at the bank."

"No sweat. You stay with Mike. He's alone, and he'll need all the support he can get."

Freeman left with Wainwright. The mayor put his arm around McCarthy and assured him of the city's support. "Everyone loves Angel. I wouldn't want to be in the kidnapper's shoes if anything happens to her. You tell Mike that we're at his disposal. The whole damn city's at his disposal."

"That'll help."

They left McCarthy with Masuto, who said, "You'll forgive me if my questions are blunt. I have to get home and change clothes, and I want to get to Barton's as early as possible. First —how much is the ransom?"

"A million dollars."

"Has Barton got it?"

"He'll get it. Yes, he's got it."

"When did the kidnapping take place?"

McCarthy stared at Masuto thoughtfully for a long moment

before answering. "They say you're good. Are you that good?"

"I'm a cop," Masuto said. "I do my job."

"That's fair enough. The Bartons have a place out at Malibu. Last night there was a party at the Malibu Colony. Mike felt rotten, headache, maybe a touch of the flu. He talked Angel into going without him, and he told her that if it got to be past midnight and she was enjoying herself, she shouldn't try to drive home but stay over at their Malibu place and come in today."

"That sounds like an understanding husband."

"They have a good relationship. Mike went to sleep. At three in the morning he was awakened by the kidnapper's call. The man told Mike he had Angel and that the ransom was a million."

"Who gave the party?"

"Netty Cooper. She was married to Sam Cooper, the producer. They're divorced. She got the house at Malibu."

"What did Barton do then?"

"He drove out to Malibu. His house had been broken into. There were signs of a struggle—broken lamps, overturned chairs."

"Did he then go over to Cooper's place?"

"No. The kidnapper had warned him to keep it quiet. For all Mike knew, the party might still be going on."

"Is his house in the Colony?"

"No, about a mile away."

"He's a cool-headed man."

"Yes, he is."

"And what was his next move?" Masuto asked.

"He telephoned me from the beach house and I met him here at his home in Beverly Hills. It was about six o'clock in the morning then. I persuaded him to call Al Freeman. The kidnapper had been very emphatic about what would happen to Angel if he communicated with the police, but Al felt he must call in the feds. Then I talked to Bill Ranier. A million dollars in cash is a very large order, Sergeant. No one bank carries that kind of cash. Fortunately, both Bill and I have good connections with a number of banks."

"But you found the cash?"

"It's promised. It's being put together and it will be delivered to the Central Bank of Los Angeles by nine-thirty. I'll pick it up there. The kidnapper said he'll call in his instructions for the drop at noon."

"Did Barton talk to his wife when the kidnapper called?"

"Oh, yes."

"What did she say?"

"She was frightened. Mike says she could hardly talk. What does a woman say in a situation like that?"

"If he repeated her exact words and if you can remember them, I'd like to hear them."

"What difference does it make? Time is running out."

"It might be important."

McCarthy shook his head and knit his brow. "I don't know. 'Help me.' I think. 'Get me out of this, please, Mike.' Something like that. I didn't press him."

"Do they have a security system in their house at Malibu?"

"I think so, yes."

"It connects with the Malibu police?"

"I really don't know." He looked at his watch. "Suppose you hold the rest of your questions for Mike when you get out there. I have to get over to the bank."

Masuto nodded, and as McCarthy left, Wainwright entered the room. "The gardener's rig will be downstairs in a few minutes, Masao. I swear I don't like this. It's lousy police method, and the feds are leaning on us and screaming special privilege. What in hell do they expect? It's Beverly Hills not Hell's Kitchen. There's more weight in this town than at a fat farm, and it all leans on us."

"When he goes to make the drop," Masuto said, "should I try to follow him?"

"No. We have to leave him clear."

"I don't like it. It's wrong."

"I know. It's lousy police work."

"I don't mean that," Masuto said. "It's wrong on his end."

"What does that mean?"

"I don't know. It just doesn't wash."

"Sure. And when you get something more than one of your goddamn Oriental hunches, I'll talk about it. Meanwhile, keep an eye out for my car."

"What do you mean, keep an eye out for your car?"

"My car was stolen. Didn't Beckman tell you? My car—right here in Beverly Hills, standing in the driveway of my house."

"That is adding insult to injury. Still, Captain, if you insist on driving a Mercedes, you take the risk that goes with it."

"What do you mean, Mercedes? The car's twelve years old. I bought it for nine hundred dollars and put three thousand into it. Sure it's a Mercedes—ah, the hell with it! We'll find it. Meanwhile, get into some old clothes and look like a gardener."

"I am a gardener," Masuto replied as he opened the door to leave. "I grow the best roses, the best tomatoes, and the best cucumbers in Los Angeles. It's a relief to pretend to be something I understand."

Masuto stopped to look into his office, where Beckman still labored over the files. "I hear you've turned gardener," Beckman said.

"I wish it were permanent. What have you got?"

"Not much, but Mike Barton is an interesting guy. Angel isn't her name and Barton isn't his."

"What is his name?"

"I'm not absolutely certain, but maybe it's Brannigan. Also, he gambles."

"Everyone gambles."

"Big. Also, which I'm not sure about either, cocaine, and maybe the Angel sniffs a bit as well."

"Can you find anything on her?"

"I'm looking."

"Keep looking. From what I'm told, the drop will take place at twelve noon. This has to be kept very quiet, but the big brass convinced Wainwright to leave him uncovered when he makes the drop."

"That's crazy!" Beckman exclaimed.

"Maybe yes, maybe no. I don't think it makes much difference. I'll see you later."

The gardener's truck was downstairs, an old Ford pickup with two lawnmowers sitting in the loading area. There were also picks, shovels, two bags of lime and a rolled-up hose. It had a cranky clutch and it bucked as Masuto backed out of the parking area.

It was just nine o'clock when he parked the pickup in front of his house in Culver City. Unlike New York City, there was no regulation requiring Beverly Hills policemen to live in Beverly Hills. If there had been, they would have to have been very wealthy policemen indeed. The small cottage in Culver City, only a few miles from Beverly Hills, was Masuto's base, his retreat, his argument that the world he lived in was not entirely insane and bloodthirsty. There was his home, his wife, his children, his tiny meditation room and his rose garden. Now his children were at school, the teen-age burglar had departed and evidently his wife, Kati, was out shopping, for the house was empty. He changed into old shoes, work pants, and a blue shirt, and as he was ready to leave, Kati entered, her arms full. Masuto took the bags of groceries from her and carried them into the kitchen, while Kati told him how delighted she was that he had been given the day off and was prepared to work in his garden.

"I am not going to work in the garden. In two minutes, I shall drive off in that truck parked in front of the house."

"The gardener's truck?"

"Yes."

Kati shook her head bewilderedly.

"I have not become a gardener. It's a costume for my assignment. I'll tell you about it tonight. Until then—" He spread his hands.

"Ah, so. We are man and wife, but still I'm not to be trusted. Very old Japanese, Masao," she said, shaking her head. Kati was the gentlest of souls, but since she had joined a group of nisei women in the process of consciousness raising, she had developed a vocabulary of protest and disapproval. "Old Japanese" was a part of it. Masuto kissed her, refused to argue the point, and left the house, reflecting that as a Zen Buddhist he was poorly developed indeed. He should have been able to see her point of view. Well, one day he would change all that—one day when he had completed his twenty-two years on the force and was in a position to receive his pension. When that time came, he would spend at least six hours a day in meditation in the Zendo in downtown Los Angeles. Until then, unfortunately, he was a policeman.

Or was he just that, a policeman and no more? What was the point, the focus of his existence? With all his years of meditation, he had not experienced enlightenment, or satori, as the Japanese called it. He was more romantically inclined than people suspected. His wife, Kati, knew that her husband was a most unusual man, but even she did not suspect that there were times when he saw himself as a member of the ancient samurai. That was sheer fantasy. His family was not of the samurai, but out of plain peasant people, for all their success here in this new country; but at a moment in history Zen Buddhism had been the religion of the samurai, and for all of his failings, Masuto was a Zen Buddhist—and how so different from the samurai? The film the Japanese had made, which was titled *The Seven Samurai*, fascinated Masuto. He had seen it three times, brooding over the mentality of these seven men who must save a village, even at the cost of their lives, a village where they had no connection—except perhaps the human connection. That was very Zen.

And was that why he lived out the role of a policeman?

Or did he live simply for the occasional puzzle that broke up the dull routine of robberies? In all truth, he loved his work. That was his burden, his karma, to make his life out of the bleakest, the most horrifying aspects of what is euphemistically called civilization. Be that as it may, his problem now was to go disguised as a Japanese gardener, to the home of a film star, and to try to find out why said film star was unwilling to involve the police in the kidnapping of his wife. Wainwright would have seen it differently; he would have insisted that Masuto's responsibility was to find the kidnapper and to protect Angel Barton—if, conceivably, she could be protected. Why, Masuto wondered, did a part of his own mind reject that notion?

Then he put his thoughts aside. It was best not to think, not to speculate. More must happen.

Mike Barton's home was on Whittier Drive, north of Sunset Boulevard, at the extreme western edge of Beverly Hills. In a wealthy and elegant city, this was one of the wealthier and more elegant neighborhoods, enormous houses of twenty and thirty rooms sitting in manicured jungles of exotic tropical plantings. Barton's house suited the neighborhood, a strange combination of oversized Irish cottage and French chateau, painted white, surrounded by a whitewashed stone wall. A high iron gate opened to the driveway, and as Masuto turned into the entrance, the gate opened, indicating that someone was expecting him and had noted his approach. He drove around to the back of the house, as a gardener would, and as he got out of the car, Bill Ranier, Barton's business manager, came out of the back door to meet him.

"All right, Sergeant, you're here," Ranier said. "I don't know how good this idea is, but since your people insist, Mike agreed to go along with it. Just remember that he's pretty damn disturbed, so don't try to break him down. He's going to do this his own way, and any pressure or strongarm tactics can only hurt Angel—maybe kill her."

"I don't use strongarm tactics," Masuto said softly, "but it might be worth noting that in Italy, where the payment of ransom is forbidden by law, people have tried to operate this way, without the police. It doesn't help. The same number of kidnap victims are killed. If Barton would cooperate, we might get both the kidnappers and his wife and a million dollars to boot."

"Well, he won't. He's going to do it his way."

"Is the money here?"

"Inside. McCarthy got here a few minutes ago."

"In what form? What kind of bills?"

"Twenties, fifties and hundreds. We have the numbers, but hell, there's no problem with laundering it. Billions of petrodollars floating around the world, so I guess we can kiss it good-bye."

"Possibly. I think now I'd like to talk to Barton. By the way, how many servants are in the house?"

"He keeps three in help, Joe Kelly chauffeurs and doubles as a butler when he has to, Freda Holtz—she's the cook—and Lena Jones, the maid."

"Does Kelly do the gardening?"

"No, Mexican gardener comes in twice a week, not today. Now look, here's the scenario we worked out. I tell Mike you're here. He yells and puts up a fuss. I calm him and tell him he might as well talk to you. That's for any big ears. I tell him it will help to pass the time and ease the waiting. Then he comes outside and walks with you through the plantings. He's got a small greenhouse at the other end of the property, so you can go in there and talk. It should make some sense to anyone who might be listening."

"You only mentioned the three in help. Are there any others?"

"Just his secretary, Elaine Newman."

"Is she here today?"

"Not yet. She comes in around ten, but she could be early or late. Mike doesn't hold her to strict hours."

"Does she know about the kidnapping?"

"No, and we decided not to tell her. When she comes in, I'll send her over to my office to get some papers and my secretary will keep her waiting there and then she has to pick up a manuscript for Mike. That will keep her out of it until noon. This is still off the record, and according to the kidnapper, we have to keep it that way."

"All right." Masuto nodded. "I'll wait right here for Barton."

2
Mike Barton

Masuto had occasionally speculated on what makes a "banka-ble" star, a term very expressive in Hollywood if nowhere else in America. Certainly it was not theatrical talent, not appearance—though appearance was important—not beauty, not brains, but rather an indefinable thing which some called charisma for want of a better name. It was not connected with the way an actor lived his life, treated the other sex, was or was not a doper, a drunk, a liar, or a thief. It was something that cut through all that, recognizable yet indefinable—and whatever it was, Mike Barton possessed it. He was onstage as he stepped out of his house, and he strode over to Masuto with a kind of assurance reserved for his narrow clan, yet lacking, Masuto felt, any of that tired inelasticity that comes from fear and sorrow. He was a star, but not a very good actor.

He shook hands and said, "Let's walk, Sergeant. My house has big ears."

"Whose ears?"

"Damned if I know."

"Kidnapping for ransom is planned. It's not decided on the

spur of the moment. Someone must have known that your wife would spend the night at the beach house."

"Who? I didn't know it myself. Angel didn't know. We decided that she should show up at the party because Netty's a dear old friend. I had a splitting headache and I felt too rotten to trek over to Malibu. I told Angel that if the party was a drag, she should cut out of there at ten o'clock or so, but if she was having fun and decided to stay on, she shouldn't try to drive back here. Hell, that's what the beach house is for."

"But the people at the party would know that she planned to stay overnight."

"Some of them, maybe. I suppose Netty would know. Where the hell is all this leading, Sergeant?"

"The woman who gave the party, Netty Cooper—did you talk to her?"

"Come on, come on. My wife was in trouble."

"Still," Masuto persisted, "someone must have known that she would be at the party—"

"Sure. People knew that."

They were at the greenhouse now. "I guess we ought to step inside," Barton said, "just in case someone's watching. It'll make some sense for me to be walking in the garden with you."

Inside the greenhouse Masuto asked him, "Who might be watching?"

"Goddamnit, Sergeant, you get me at the worst moment of my life and ask me questions that make no damn sense."

"I'm sorry."

"All I want is to get back into the house and wait for the phone to ring."

"I can understand that."

"Then it makes no sense for me to be out here talking to a gardener. You keep asking me who is watching. How the hell do I know? But someone knows every move I make and every move Angel makes, and they're going to think it's funny as hell for me to be out here with you. Furthermore, let me tell you this: If anyone follows me when I make the drop and

Angel is hurt, I swear to God I'll sue Beverly Hills for every dollar they got in their treasury."

"No one will follow you."

"Then I suggest you get your truck out of here."

Masuto nodded, reflecting that to be a policeman in Beverly Hills was quite different from being a policeman anywhere else in the world. He watched Mike Barton stride across the garden to the house, the stride and bearing of a thoroughbred horse, and then Masuto walked to his truck, got in, and drove out of the place. A few minutes later he parked the pickup at the police station on Rexford Drive, ignored a uniformed cop who wanted to know whether he had changed his profession, and then climbed the stairs to Wainwright's office.

"Back already?" Wainwright asked sourly.

"He didn't want me there. He raised hell and told me to get out."

"Great. We pay a hundred dollars to rent the truck for a day and we get ten minutes out of it."

"Beverly Hills can afford it."

"They don't pay for it. It comes out of our budget. Did you get anything?"

"Not really. Some impressions."

"Well, just sit on them. The city manager was in here and he wants us to keep hands off. Ranier and McCarthy are there with Barton, and they'll be in touch with us once Barton pays the ransom. When Angel is returned, we can move in and investigate."

"And if Angel isn't returned?"

"Let's take it one thing at a time."

"I'd like to go out to Malibu now," Masuto said.

"What for?"

"I want to see his beach house and I want to talk to Netty Cooper, the lady who gave the party where Angel spent last night."

"The Malibu cops are handling that."

"I know, Captain. Nevertheless, she resides here. The Malibu cops would expect us to stick our noses into it."

"I don't want trouble with the brass, Masao. They want us to keep hands off."

"Absolutely. I'm not tailing Barton or interfering with him. I'm looking at a place where a crime was committed, a break-in and a kidnapping. It would be derelict on our part not to look into it, and it would undoubtedly open us to various charges that—"

"All right. Do it. I'm sick of being told when to be a cop and when not to."

"I'd like to take Beckman with me."

"What for? You need the company?"

"For protection. He's bigger than I am."

"Take him and get the hell out of here!"

His desk still covered with files, Beckman was talking into the telephone when Masuto entered. He put down the phone, and Masuto told him, "Come take a ride. We'll drive over to my house, I'll change clothes, and then we'll head out to Malibu. Unless you got something out of this morning?"

"We'll talk in the car," Beckman said. He was a big man, three inches taller than Masuto's six feet, heavy-set and slope-shouldered. He sat in Masuto's old Datsun scrunched over and observed that when you scratched the surface of anyone, what came up was pretty damn strange.

"How's that?"

"You want to know about Angel. Well, I put out every line we have. I called Gloria Adams at the *L.A. Times* and I called Freda Mons at the *Examiner*. Between them they know about every celebrity in the country, when they pee and when they cut their fingernails and who they're in bed with, and I even called Elsie Binns at S.A.G., who knows practically every actor in the world, and do you know that none of them could come up with even a license tag for Angel Barton. That is, before two and a half years ago, which was when she moved in with Mike Barton. So who is she and where was she and where does she come from?"

"How about her maiden name?"

"That, Masao, is a lulu. Nobody, but nobody, has the vaguest notion what her maiden name was, or whatever her last name was, maiden or not."

"What did they call her? They must have called her something."

"They called her Angel."

"What about the Motor Vehicles Bureau?" Masuto demanded. "Did you try them? If she drove a car before she was married, she had a license."

"I'm slow but not stupid, Masao. Sure I tried them. They're a pretty lousy organization to begin with and they don't break their backs doing things for the Beverly Hills cops, and when I told them that all I had was a first name and an address, they didn't exactly applaud me. Nothing. So I called the L.A. cops who got some good computers. Zilch. Zilch wherever I turned. Two and a half years ago, that lady just didn't exist."

"She existed. Now what about Barton?"

They were at Masuto's cottage now, and Beckman suggested that they save Barton for the ride out to Malibu. "Otherwise, we got to talk about the weather, which doesn't change, and football, which ain't your game anyway."

It was after eleven now, and Kati, delighted to see her husband at midday, immediately began to prepare food. "I'm not hungry," Masuto said. "I'll change and then we'll have to go." Beckman was hungry, and Kati fried a large hamburger, which he wolfed down with a glass of milk. "I expected tempura," he explained to Masuto when they were back in the car. "You didn't expect me to pass up an offer of Kati's tempura."

"You ate hamburger."

"That's what I got. I'd have to be a pig to turn it down and ask for tempura."

"I guess you would."

It was about twenty-five miles from Masuto's home in Culver City to the old Malibu Road, the location of the Bartons' beach house. When they were on the Pacific Coast Highway heading north, Masuto reminded Beckman about Barton. "You said his real name might just be Brannigan. Why 'might just be'? A good many film actors change their names. It's no great secret."

"It is and it isn't, Masao. In the old days Jewish and Italian and Polish actors used to sit on their real names, and sometimes their real names were absolutely secret, actors like Leslie Howard and Kirk Douglas and Tony Curtis to name only a few. But after the war things changed and you got people like George Segal and Sylvester Stallone who don't give a damn and lots of others too. But with Barton, it's different."

"How's that?"

"Well, think about the way he looks, a kind of a cross between Robert Redford and Ronald Reagan. He's got to be Irish or Wasp, so you don't think of him changing his name. But his past is as blurred as the Angel's. He turned up here in Hollywood in 1964 and it seems that for two years he did everything except act—washed dishes, waited on tables, pumped gas. Then he got some bit parts in TV, and then he pulled off a major role in a series—and from there, zoom. He's one of the top ten. But who is he? Nobody seems to know."

"A hundred million people have seen his face. How does he hide?"

"Maybe he don't have to hide. You hide if you're on the run, if there's a want out for you. If it's just a background you're maybe ashamed of, or some kind of nastiness that won't help the image, or maybe even something you want to forget, you change your name."

"Then where did the Brannigan notion come from?" Masuto reminded him.

"I talked to Gloria Adams at the *L.A. Times*. She says that in the interviews with fan magazines and such, Barton just blurs his past—admits to being an Easterner from upstate New York, but she mentioned that two years ago she got a letter from back East. She tells me her column is syndicated all over the country, and this letter says that Barton's real name is Brannigan and that he comes from Schenectady in New York. So she asked Barton, and he says it's a lot of hogwash, so she just forgot about it, because crazy mail is a part of her job.

She wanted to know how come the Beverly Hills cops were suddenly interested in Mike Barton, but I put her off and told her that if something broke, she'd be the first to know."

"Did you call the Schenectady cops?"

"I did that, but they don't have fancy computers, and they said that for anything seventeen or eighteen years ago it would take a couple of days to get into their old files."

Masuto nodded. "That's good work, Sy. From here on we'll just take it as it comes."

"You think he'll ever see Angel again?"

"Somehow, I do."

"It's almost noon. By now Barton's made the drop."

"I would presume so."

It was just past twelve when they turned left off the Pacific Coast Highway at old Malibu Road and pulled up in front of the Malibu police station. Joe Cominsky, the Malibu chief of police, had started out as a uniformed cop with Sy Beckman when they were both members of the Los Angeles police, and now he shook his hand warmly. "It's been a long time, Sy, many moons."

"I envy you. If you've got to be a cop, I suppose Malibu's got everything else beat."

"It has its points. Glad to meet you, Sergeant," he said to Masuto. "Maybe you're just what we need on this, because this Barton thing is sure as hell a Chinese puzzle."

"The sergeant's not Chinese. He's nisei."

"I know, I know. Just an expression. No offense."

"Forget it," Masuto said. "I know what you mean. I'd like to look at their beach house, and then I'd like to talk to Netty Cooper. I'm sure you've been talking to her."

"Just got back from there."

"Then you have a list of the guests last night?"

"It's a Who's Who of the film business. You know the kind of people we got out here in the Malibu Colony. Top directors, top stars, top producers. The thought of a couple of them sneaking down the road after the party to kidnap Angel Barton is just bananas."

"Were there no people from outside the Colony?"

"Fred Simmons, the producer, and his wife. Simmons is sixty-seven with a bad ticker. They left about eleven. Fred Simmons has more millions than you could shake a stick at. He's no candidate."

"How many people were there?"

"About twenty altogether."

"I'd like to talk to Mrs. Cooper."

"Absolutely," Cominsky said.

"And to have a look at the Bartons' beach house."

"Sure. Suppose we go along there now. I'd like another opinion. When I said Chinese puzzle before, I wasn't making an ethnic crack. I meant the puzzle part of it. It's just a mile down old Malibu Road. I'll drive you there."

"Then Angel never had to touch the highway. She just drove down Malibu Road. I suppose someone could have been waiting, watching for her car."

When they reached the Barton beach house, Cominsky pointed to the slope on the inland side facing the house. "Nothing there but mustard grass. No place to hide."

"On top?"

"Maybe. There's a road up there, between here and the Pacific Coast Highway, so I guess they could have parked there and watched. But let's look at the house."

The house was one-story and brown-shingled, presenting a blank wall to the road. The entrance was on the beach side, and alongside the house, nestled between the Barton house and the adjoining house, an alley led through to the beach. Cominsky opened the door to the alley, explaining, "Most of the people here leave passkeys with us."

"No garage?" Masuto asked.

"Not here. Very few of them. People park in the space in front of their houses."

"I don't see her car?"

"They took it—a yellow two-seat Mercedes. Worth over forty grand. We put out an APB on it, but no word yet."

"And when they left, was the gate open?"

"Right. Hold that thought, Sergeant. The gate wasn't jim-
mied. Either they opened it with a passkey, or they came
around from the beach. And the nearest public pass-through
to the beach is a quarter of a mile away. Just follow me
through here."

The passageway was no more than three feet wide, the
house directly on the left making a windowless wall. In the
Bartons' house there were several side windows, all of them
covered with fretted iron grillwork.

"What about these people next door?" Masuto asked.

"Divorced actor. He does westerns in Spain. Been there
three months and not expected back until next month."

They emerged into the blazing sunlight of Malibu Beach,
the white sand stretching in front of them, a man walking a
dog, a youngster in a wet suit trying to surf, and four pretty
girls playing volleyball. The Barton house had a broad shaded
porch facing the ocean, and in front of it and three steps
down, a wooden terrace enclosed by a picket fence. On the
terrace were tables under striped beach umbrellas—folded
now—lounge chairs, and dining chairs. Cominsky opened the
gate at the side of the picket fence and led them across the
terrace.

"Barred on the road side, but not the beach side."

"The water kills thoughts of evil," Masuto said, and Cominsky glanced at him strangely.

"Yet the evil persists," Masuto added, smiling. "Only the
sand is washed clean. Forgive me, Chief. I'm also puzzled."

"Oh? Yeah," Cominsky agreed. "Just take a look at this
front door." He unlocked a police padlock that had been
bolted to the door and stood aside. Masuto and Beckman
stared at the door, which had been attacked in two places by
a jimmy and forced open. In the lower corner of the window,
next to the door, was a stick-on label with the legend HELMS
SECURITY.

"Helms ties into police stations," Masuto said. "Was this
tied into yours?"

"You're damn right, Sergeant."

"You tested it? It was working?"

"Absolutely."

"And you had someone on duty?" Masuto persisted.

"Even if we didn't, there's an alarm bell attached that can be heard a mile away on this beach."

"In other words," said Beckman, "she never turned on the alarm."

"Come inside."

They stood in the living room of the attractively furnished cottage—grass rug, wicker furniture with bright blue upholstery, good prints on the walls. Masuto stood staring, captivated. Two of the prints were askew, a lamp was knocked over and smashed, a chair was turned over, and the grass rug was pulled out of place.

"I want you to see the bedroom," Cominsky said.

"In a moment." He was trying to recreate a struggle in his mind and fit it into what had happened in the room. Beckman, who knew him well, watched with interest. "All right," Masuto said.

"There are three bedrooms." Cominsky led the way. "This is the master."

The bedclothes were rumpled, a nightgown on the floor. As Masuto studied the scene, Cominsky walked over and touched a switch next to the bed. Above the switch, a red light glowed.

"This is the alarm switch. The light's on when the switch is off."

"I should think it would be the other way," Beckman said.

"No, this makes sense. You put out the lights, and then the red light reminds you about the alarm."

"What time did she leave the party?" Masuto asked.

"About one A.M. When they all live in the Colony, the parties tend to run late."

"But it was a weekday. Most of them would have to be in the studios very early."

"Yeah. She was one of the last to leave."

"And Barton got the call at three A.M. That leaves two hours. Unless they were stupid enough to make the call from here, they had to break in and take her somewhere. If they were watching her, why didn't they intercept her? Why break in at all? And if she went straight to bed, why didn't she reach out and turn on the alarm?"

"You tell me," Cominsky said.

"And if she wasn't asleep, why didn't she reach out and turn on the alarm when she heard the door go?"

"Was the bedside lamp on?" Masuto asked.

"It was."

"You had the place dusted?"

"Early this morning. We don't look for anything there."

"Can I use the phone?"

"Be my guest."

He called Beverly Hills and got through to Wainwright. "It's one o'clock," Masuto said. "What do you hear from Barton?"

"Nothing."

"Did he pay the ransom?"

"According to Ranier he got the call from the kidnappers over an hour ago and left just before noon, taking the million dollars with him."

"Never said where he was going?"

"Not a word."

"Did Ranier listen in on an extension?" Masuto asked.

"He says he didn't. He's there with McCarthy, waiting for Barton to show. Where are you?"

"At Barton's beach house."

"Did you find anything?"

"Confusion. I'd like to talk to Netty Cooper while I'm out here."

"Why not? Aside from the confusion, you got any ideas, Masuto?"

"Too many. If you want me, you can call the Malibu station. They're right outside the Colony."

He put down the phone and turned to Cominsky, who asked him if he had seen enough.

"I think so." He picked up the nightgown and looked at it—

white silk, white lace. He put it to his face to smell it. Cominsky grinned. Beckman said, "I never knew you went in for that, Masao."

"Only lately."

Cominsky padlocked the cottage door again.

"If the system is turned on with the bedside switch," Masuto said, "then what happens when you open the door from the outside?"

"There's a switch in the lock that turns it off. It's not foolproof, but it's a damn hard lock to pick."

"Does your screen at the police station tell you when the alarm systems are on or off?"

"Yes. The officer on duty says it was off."

"Here on this part of the old road," Masuto said, "what kind of people live here?"

"Mostly the same kind you find in the Colony down the road, only with less money for the most part. Of course, some of them, like Barton, use their houses only on weekends, and some of the houses, like this one, are as classy as the houses in the Colony. Some people don't want to live in the Colony, and then the houses at the Colony aren't for sale very often. You get writers, actors, directors, lawyers—you name it."

Masuto turned toward the ocean, staring at the incoming waves, apparently lost in thought. "I'd like to live here," Beckman said. "I guess I'd rather live here than anywhere else."

"Time was, and not so long ago," Cominsky told them, "that you could buy one of these houses for forty, fifty thousand dollars. Now there isn't one you can touch for less than half a million."

Masuto smiled thinly and shrugged. "Let's go back to the station house." He had been thinking that Malibu Beach was very beautiful. But most of the world was very beautiful until men touched it.

3

Malibu Beach

Back at the Malibu police station, Masuto found a message to call Wainwright at the Beverly Hills station. He made the call and was put through to Wainwright, who said, "What was taken has been returned."

"Very cryptic and interesting."

"I got a room full of reporters. I'll call you back in five minutes."

Masuto put down the telephone and asked Cominsky, "How much has this leaked?"

"Who knows, Masuto? I did my best. The local news people were here. They always are when there's a break-in on the beach, but I didn't say word one about kidnapping. They wanted to know were any of the Bartons in the house. I had no comment for that."

"What about Netty Cooper?"

"She had to know something was going on when I got the list of her guests. But I didn't mention the kidnapping. That won't help. It'll come out before the day's over."

"Angel's back."

"How do you know?" Beckman asked him.

"I spoke to Wainwright. He had a room full of reporters. I guess that means it'll be out. The chief's right. You can't sit on something like that."

"Well, thank God," Cominsky said. "She's a nice lady. I'd hate to think that anything happened to her. Is she all right? Did they rough her up?"

"I don't know. Wainwright didn't fill me in on any details."

"I'm starved," Beckman said.

"You can grab a bite at the drugstore in the shopping center across the road. It's not great, but it's all right. Or you can drive down to the pier and eat fancy."

"We have to wait for Wainwright to call back."

A few minutes later the call from Wainwright came through. "Masao," he said, "I'll be leaving for Mike Barton's place in about an hour, and I want you to meet me there."

"You said his wife is back?"

"Right. No harm done except some tape marks on her mouth and wrists. She says she was snatched out of her Malibu house by two men who wore stocking masks, taken somewhere, and finally dumped on Mulholland Drive, just to the west of the Coldwater Canyon. She walked to the firehouse and they drove her home. McCarthy's with her, and that's the story he tells me. I got to meet with the mayor and city manager again, because they think they can sit on this and I got to tell them they're crazy."

"What about Mike Barton?"

"No sign of him yet."

"Did you put out anything on him? He should be back by now."

"Not yet, Masao. You know, he could have made the drop fifty miles from here. The kidnappers could have split up. One takes Angel, one goes to pick up the money. What are you thinking?"

"I don't know exactly what I'm thinking," Masuto said. "It's nothing I can put my finger on. It's just a smell. It doesn't smell right."

"No, it stinks, and I don't know why either, except when

there's a crime and people tell the cops to keep hands off, well, that stinks for me."

"Who else is at his house?"

"Ranier's still there, and there's a uniformed cop I just sent over and told to sit in his car on the street, and if they don't like that, they can stuff it. What did you find in their beach house?"

"Puzzles. Questions."

"You might go straight to Barton's place."

"Well, we're here, so we might as well talk to Netty Cooper who had the party here last night. It's one-thirty now. I should be able to get to Barton's place by three or a little later."

"Okay. I'll meet you there."

"Try to hold McCarthy and Ranier there. Also the three servants and a woman called Elaine Newman. She's his secretary."

"Hold on, Masao. We can't detain anyone. You know that."

"Just ask them, politely."

"I'll try. But we got nothing to detain anyone on."

"We're not arresting them. All I want to do is talk to them."

"I'll try."

They stopped at the drugstore where Masuto ordered a bacon and tomato sandwich and Beckman ordered ham and cheese on rye. "Didn't you just eat lunch at my house?" Masuto asked him.

"Sure, but that was a long time ago."

"Yes, I suppose it was."

It was only a couple of hundred yards from the police station to the gate to Malibu Colony. At that point, where one turns off the Pacific Coast Highway to the old Malibu Road, the Colony is directly to one's left, a manned gate, and then beyond it a row of some of the most expensive houses in southern California. Masuto had frequently reflected on the lot of a detective trying to juggle the payment of bills, mortgage, doctor, dentist, grocery, insurance, etc., on a policeman's salary while protecting people who earned more in one year than a policeman could earn in a lifetime.

At the Colony gate, the guard looked at Masuto's identification and shook his head. "Heavy today—heaviest day we had in a long time. First the local fuzz and now fancy Beverly Hills cops. What goes on?"

Masuto shrugged.

"Come on, I'm on your side."

"The creature came out of the sea," Beckman said.

"Funny, funny."

"Which is Mrs. Cooper's house?"

"Down there. You can't miss it, painted bright yellow."

They drove through and parked in front of the yellow house. A Chicano maid opened the door and asked them to wait. In a few minutes she returned and asked them to follow her. Unlike the Barton house, this one had a proper entrance facing the road. It was two stories, had striped awnings, an entrance way, a huge living room-dining room with baroque furniture painted white, and, facing the sea, tall glass sliding doors. Netty Cooper was sitting on the deck-terrace with a man—a tall, elegant, good-looking man of about fifty. He was dressed in gray flannels, sported a carefully combed and barbered head of iron gray hair with pale gray eyes to match— and a face that was vaguely familiar.

"Two Beverly Hills detectives," Netty Cooper said with obvious relish. "I never knew they had any detectives on the Beverly Hills police force, only those handsome men in uniform with the pale blue eyes, and so polite, so very polite. But you do have to be polite to be a policeman in Beverly Hills, don't you?" Her own eyes were very pale blue. She was a slender, attenuated woman in her middle forties, with a long face, long neck, long trunk, and long legs. Her dyed yellow hair was piled on her head, and her nail polish was so dark it was almost black. She wore a beach dress of pale green, and her sandals revealed toenails painted the same color as her fingernails.

"Yes, ma'am—very polite," Beckman said. Those who didn't

know Beckman and took him at his appearance, that of an oversized running back, were often surprised by his irony. Masuto was watching the man. He recognized him now, Congressman Roy Hennesy.

"And of course you've come about poor Angel's kidnapping."

"How do you know that Angel Barton was kidnapped?"

"Oh, one knows. This is a very small place. What has happened to our Angel?"

"She has been returned unharmed."

There was a pause, and then Hennesy said, "Thank God. Kidnapping is a horrible thing."

"I am Detective Sergeant Masuto. This is Detective Beckman."

"How nice! How very nice! And this is Congressman Hennesy, a dear friend. Masuto. How nice to think that we have a Japanese detective on the Beverly Hills police force. I spent three months in Japan, and I would love to chat about it. So many things I didn't understand. You could be so helpful."

"I'm afraid not, I've never been to Japan."

"Really? Then you must go."

"Yes. Thank you for the suggestion. Meanwhile, I'm much more interested in the Barton kidnapping."

"Oh? Are we on the list of suspects?"

"So sorry," Masuto said, "we have no suspects but would appreciate information."

Beckman watched him narrowly. Masuto rarely displayed anger, but when he fell into what Wainwright called his Charlie Chan routine, he was provoked and dangerous.

"How disappointing! I always wanted to be a suspect."

"Were you at the party last night?" he asked Hennesy.

"I was. But I assure you, I did not kidnap the Angel. If I had, I would never return her. I would give up my seat in Congress and find a desert island somewhere—a place where she and I could live out our lives in idyllic ecstasy."

"Ah, so. And does she feel that way about you?"

"Sergeant, must you be so literal? Half the men in Los Angeles are in love with the Angel," Mrs. Cooper said, and then to Hennesy, "but you are a very heartless man to sit there and tell me you dream of running off with the Angel."

"My apologies, and the disclaimer must include the fact that I am here with you, while the Angel snuggles in the arms of her devoted husband. How devoted, I wonder? How much was the ransom, Sergeant?"

"I have no idea," Masuto said.

"Close-mouthed—ah, well, an officer in pursuit of his duty."

"Did you leave the party before or after Mrs. Barton?"

"I really don't know."

"You mean with all your talk about a desert island, you didn't notice whether she was gone or not?"

"She left before Mr. Hennesy did," Mrs. Cooper told him. "I don't think any of my guests were candidates for a kidnapping—Jack Fellows and his wife, more millions than they know what to do with, the Tudors—well, a star does not dash around kidnapping people—Kennedy, only the most successful director in town, the Butterworths and the Goldbergs and the Lees. Not a very large party, Mr. Detective, and no one who is a potential for your kidnapper. If you think that any of my guests walked out of here and went over to the Barton place and kidnapped Angel Barton, you are absolutely out of your mind."

Masuto stared at her for a long moment; then he nodded.

"We'll be going now—oh, one thing. Which of your guests live in the Colony?"

"The Lees and the Goldbergs. Are you going to grill them as well?"

"I haven't grilled you, Mrs. Cooper."

"The Goldbergs are four houses down, the Lees are the sixth house."

"And, Congressman, when did you first learn about the kidnapping?"

"About two minutes before you arrived, Sergeant. I've been here about an hour, but Mrs. Cooper was upstairs doing her bath and things. I walked around to the beach side and made myself comfortable on the terrace. We're old pals. And, by the way, I didn't think you were serious about who left first, and I was rather put off by your questioning me. I did leave before Angel, if that matters."

"Thank you," Masuto said coldly.

Outside, Beckman let out his breath and shook his head. "They are a pair. She's a normal Beverly Hills type phony. The congressman's a fuckin' pain in the ass. They almost had an indictment out on him once, and then it was squashed, and they go on reelecting him. You want to keep your hands in your pockets if you get close to him."

"What now?" Masuto asked him. "The Lees or the Goldbergs?"

"Let's give the Goldbergs a shot."

The Goldberg house was painted pink. Mrs. Goldberg was small, with dark hair, dark eyes, fiftyish, and had a schoolgirl figure and a good coat of tan. Her house was furnished in beach baroque, apparently de rigueur in the Colony, but with accents of pink. She asked them to sit down on the pink chairs on the terrace and poured Cokes for each of them.

"How exciting to have two real live detectives here. Wait till Joe gets home and I give him a blow by blow. Only poor Angel—"

"She's safe, Mrs. Goldberg. She's home, unharmed."

"Oh? Then I'll be bitchy and rescind my sympathy."

"I take it you don't like her?"

"Ugh! You see, I don't hide my feelings."

"That sounds like very strong feeling."

"It is. You see, Detective Masuto—that is it, Masuto?"

"Yes, indeed. And this is Detective Beckman."

"You see, I wasn't born to this sun-drenched, orange-ridden, never-never land. Joe and I made it the hard way, and he's just about the best producer in the business, so I don't have to be a diplomat, or an ass-licker, whichever you prefer. Now this is not a place without its gonifs and stinkers, as I'm sure you know, but this Angel is a beauty. Yes, indeed—even for the film business." She stopped and shook her head. "But I'm sure you're not interested in Angel."

"But we are. Please go on."

"Where do I start and where do I stop? Don't ask me to go into Angel Barton on my own. Ask me questions."

"All right. We've just come from Netty Cooper's house. She told us that you and your husband were at the party last night."

"We were. Netty's all right. She just keeps hurting all over with rejected-woman syndromes, three divorces—but since we're a community-property state, she's done brilliantly financially. Joe says she's worth at least five million."

She has fangs and she's no one's fool, Masuto reflected, asking her, "How did you find out about the kidnapping?"

"Sergeant, Joe, my husband, is producing Mikey's new film. In this kind of trouble, he would tell Joe before he told his own mother. Mikey isn't poor, but to put together a million dollars in a few hours is not easy. Joe always maintains a large liquid position, just in case he wants to tie up some literary property or a director. Joe was able to put his hands on two hundred thousand or so, and with Bill Ranier and Jack McCarthy pitching in, they were able to supply what Mikey needed for the ransom. But a million dollars for the Angel—ah well—"

"You keep saying Mikey," Beckman put in. "You must be very close to Mike Barton."

"He's like a son to us. Joe ran into him over in West Hollywood one day, pumping gas. You see—" She paused. "You see, I want to tell you this because I just don't like the smell of what's happening here, and both of you look like decent men. But please don't blow it all over town. Joe went to great effort to give Mikey a certain aura. So if this can be just among us?"

"I'll try," Masuto agreed. "We're involved with a crime, so I can't promise anything. But we'll try."

"Good enough. Mikey's father had a grocery store in Flatbush. That's in Brooklyn. We knew his father and we knew Mikey as a kid. His name then was Bernstein."

"You're kidding," Beckman said. "You mean he's Jewish?"

"What's so strange? You're Jewish, aren't you?"

"I look it."

"No law says you have to."

"And what about this rumor that his real name was Brannigan and that he came from upstate New York?"

"If you read Gloria Adams, you'll find a lot of rumors. When Joe and I were living in Flatbush and trying to make it the hard way, I saw Mikey every day, the sweetest, most willing, most decent kid I ever knew. The only kinkiness in him was that he wanted to be an actor. Then we came out to the Coast and lost touch with him, and then one day, about sixteen years ago, Joe met him at a gas pump. He brought the kid home, and we fed him and made him stay with us. Joe got him a part in a TV film, and he liked what he saw and got him an acting coach. From there on it was step by step, until he became the Mike Barton of today. We love Mikey, so I don't want to put Joe on a pedestal as Mr. Good Guy, but without Joe he would be another of the ten thousand unemployed actors around town. I don't say Joe didn't profit. He made eight films with Mikey, and six were enormous moneymakers. But that's not why he did it."

"He had already changed his name to Barton when your husband met him?"

"Yes. He wanted it that way, and Joe let it stay. They decided on a mysterious past, and it worked, for what it's worth."

"And how did he meet Angel?"

"That's another well-kept secret—" She hesitated, studying Masuto and Beckman thoughtfully.

"But you're going to tell me," Masuto said deliberately. "You're not a chatterer, but you've decided to tell me a number of things. May I ask why?"

"Is why important?"

"I think so."

"I'm afraid. There's something happening here ever since Mikey married her, and it frightens me. He's changed. A lot of stars and semi-stars in this town cat around like they're in competition. Mikey wasn't that way. There were a few girls in his life whom he really cared for, but he didn't marry until he met Angel. He lived with one lady for five years, and while they were together he never looked at another woman. He has one real weakness—one, maybe a dozen. Who hasn't? Mikey wouldn't win any prizes for smarts. He's sweet and kind, but not too bright. But the one real weakness I'm talking about is gambling. It's a sickness, and he's a big loser. He met Angel in Vegas, where she was dealing blackjack, and he fell for her like a ton of bricks. She had been on the job only a few days, and already she had the reputation of wanting nothing to do with any of the studs around the place. She walked off the job with him the next day and they came back to L.A. together and she moved in—and it didn't work, not one little bit. It was a rotten, screwed-up marriage from the word go."

"Not according to the media," Beckman said.

"You can talk to the media or you can talk to me. The Angel that the fan magazines write about—the sweet, gentle, compassionate creature—doesn't exist. The real Angel is by no means a sweet, warm woman. She's a controlled cake of ice."

"They say she has a slight foreign accent."

"She's French. She claims to have learned her English dealing at Collingwood's in London."

"Which you don't believe?"

"Joe's been to Collingwood's. He says they don't have lady dealers."

"If the marriage is so bad," Masuto asked her, "why do they stay together?"

"You never met Mikey?"

"This morning. I talked with him at his house."

"All right. He paid a million dollars for her. He adores her, pays his price, and gets nothing, absolutely nothing, in return. If you want reasons, talk to a psychiatrist. It's nothing I understand, nothing Joe understands. If she told Mikey to lay down at the front door so she could use him as a doormat,

he'd do it. The one real fight Joe ever had with Mikey was
when Mikey wanted him to put Angel into a picture."

"Why?" Beckman asked. "She's beautiful."

"Beautiful, Mr. Beckman," she said patiently, "is a salable
commodity in Grand Rapids or St. Louis. In Hollywood you
can't give it away. On any street in West Hollywood, you'll
see ten girls as beautiful as Angel, and if you walk through
one of the studios, you'll see a hundred. Of course, they don't
have her press, which comes from being married to Mikey."

"Still, if Mike Barton wanted it—"

"When you have ten million dollars riding on a picture, you
don't make gifts of starring roles. Anyway, Joe agrees with
me. She can work her charm in a living room, but she's not
enough of a woman to make it on the screen."

"What exactly do you mean?"

"I don't really know what I mean. I'm Jewish. I look at Detective Beckman here and decide that he's Jewish. Maybe if I
wasn't Jewish I wouldn't know. I'm a woman, and when I look
at Angel and talk to her—well, something's missing. It's just a
feeling. I can be very nasty when I put my mind to it."

"One more thing, if you can still put up with our questions.
At the party last night, who left first, Angel or Congressman
Hennesy?"

"They left together."

"You're sure?"

"Quite sure. But if you think Hennesy's involved in the kidnapping—no. It's not his style. He's a white-collar crook—
payoffs, bribes, influence peddling."

"You seem to know him."

"Ah, Detective Masuto, you live here in the Colony, and
you know a great many people, some nice, some not nice at
all."

"Where does Hennesy live?"

"A few miles from here."

"Is he wealthy?"

"That's hard to say. You see, a public servant is always so

ready to sell at almost any price that it's difficult to say whether poverty or larceny is the motivating factor."

Masuto nodded, repressing a smile. "Thank you. You've been very helpful and informative."

"How often do we get two good-looking city detectives out here in Malibu?"

"Even if you do look Jewish," Masuto said to Beckman when they were outside in the car.

"She's a tough little lady. I wouldn't want to get on the wrong side of her."

"Still, it's puzzling," Masuto said. "One loves Angel, one hates Angel. Nobody gives any reason why."

"You're going to look for reasons why a dumbbell falls in love, you got to be crazy."

"You think he's a dumbbell?"

"She does. She may love him like a son, but she don't give him even passing marks. Anyway, Masao, I think that as far as we're concerned, the case is closed. The feds will step in, and they want all the cards where a kidnapping is involved. Anyway, the break-in part of it and the snatch itself was in Malibu, so it drops into the lap of the Malibu cops. We might as well head back to Beverly Hills to Barton's place, and then I can tell my wife I actually saw Mike Barton in the flesh. That'll give her meat for the coffee klatch for the next two weeks. Unless you want to talk to Lee?"

"He's a screenwriter, isn't he?"

Beckman consulted his notes. "That's right. Cominsky says he's the hottest writer in the business."

"We'll skip him. I don't want any more imagination. I already have too many notions of what happened here last night."

They were on Sunset Boulevard, heading east toward Beverly Hills, when Masuto's radio lit up. It was Polly at the switchboard at the station house.

"Where are you?" she asked him.

"Just east of Sepulveda."

"Let me try to patch you through to the captain. He's been trying to get you."

"Masao?" Wainwright's voice was flat and bleak. "Where the hell are you?"

"Just passing the university."

"Well, get your ass over here to San Yisidro, just up from Tower."

"Why?"

"Because Mike Barton is sitting here in his car with a bullet through his head."

4

San Yisidro

San Yisidro is a road that winds up into the Santa Monica Hills, branching off from Tower Road a short distance from Benedict Canyon. For about a mile and a quarter San Yisidro is within the city limits of Beverly Hills, and then the road goes on into Los Angeles. It must be noted that Beverly Hills itself is an island, entirely surrounded, not by water but by the City of Los Angeles. San Yisidro is a very elegant neighborhood, but there are spots where the cactus and the mesquite still grow untouched as they have for the past hundreds of years.

It was at one such spot that Mike Barton's black Mercedes was parked, drawn up on the shoulder of the road, the central attraction for two Beverly Hills police cars: Wainwright's car and Dr. Sam Baxter's car. A uniformed policeman stood in the road, waving the curious by. Masuto and Beckman parked behind a prowl car and then joined Wainwright at the Mercedes. The door was open, and Baxter was examining the body of what had been Mike Barton. On the other side of the seat Sweeney, the Beverly Hills fingerprint man, was dusting the car and the dashboard.

"When did you find it?" Masuto asked Wainwright.

"Half hour. Officer Comdon was patrolling the road, and he saw the car. Barton looked alive just sitting there, which is why, I guess, other cars passed it by, but Comdon figured he might be lost or something."

"When was he killed?"

Wainwright nodded at Sam Baxter, and Masuto went over to the doctor and asked him.

"How the hell do I know?" Baxter snapped. "Was I here? All right, we'll play the guessing game." He looked at his watch. "It's four-thirty now. I'd say he's been dead four hours, and that's just a guess, and if you put me on a witness stand, I'll say it's a guess."

"Thank you, Doc. Next to your skill I admire your sweet nature most. What killed him?"

"A gun. What in hell do you think killed him?"

"Yes, of course," Masuto said humbly. "I thought perhaps you could tell us what kind of a gun."

"The bullet's still in his skull. When I open him up and take it out, I'll give you all the details. Meanwhile, from the entry hole, I'd guess it was a twenty-two, and since the bullet didn't go through, I'd say it was a twenty-two short. A guess, you understand? But what the hell, if I did my work the way you people do yours, my whole life would be guesses."

"Yes, our work is hardly as precise. How far away was the gun when the bullet was fired?"

"You're sure you don't want the name of the killer?"

"Only if you have it."

"The gun was no more than twelve inches away. Powder burns. If you want me to do all your work for you, I'd say that his killer was sitting in the car with him. Barton turned away, and the killer put the gun to the back of his head and fired."

"And then wiped every print from the inside of the car," Sweeney said. "Took his time and polished the inside and the door handles like he was working in a car wash."

An ambulance drew up now, and two attendants pulled a stretcher out. Beverly Hills was not large or violent enough to require its own morgue and pathology room, and they had a long-standing arrangement with All Saints Hospital for the use of both facilities. Sam Baxter, chief pathologist at All Saints, doubled as medical examiner when his services were required.

The ambulance pulled away, Baxter following it, and Wainwright, studying the car thoughtfully, asked Masuto whether he had any ideas.

"Too many." He had squatted down by the rear wheel, feeling the dirt. "It rained day before yesterday. If the killer was parked here waiting for him, there should be tracks on the shoulder in front."

Beckman anticipated him. "Right here, Masao." Wainwright and Masuto joined him. "Do you know," Masuto said wryly, "television has become an enemy. It gives the criminal the benefit of a writer's imagination." The tracks had been there, but they were deliberately scuffed out.

"Still," Beckman said, "he was parked here, which means that two cars were sitting here, and maybe people don't remember one car, but somebody's got to remember two of them."

"You know it makes no sense," Wainwright said. "It's happened enough times that kidnappers kill the kidnapped person, but why kill the man who's making the drop?"

"Yeah, why?" Beckman added.

"It makes no sense only if there *was* a kidnapping," Masuto said.

"Then what in hell was it?"

"Barton parks here to meet someone. He has a million dollars with him. The person he meets is parked in front of him. Is it a kidnapper? He doesn't tell Barton to drop the money and drive on. Instead, he leaves his car, gets into Barton's car, talks to him, and then kills him. No evidence of any struggle in the car, just a simple, friendly murder by your friendly kidnapper."

"Just hold on," Wainwright said. "If you're talking about a faked kidnapping, tell me how it makes sense. Sure Barton had to have some help to raise the million on short notice, but it's covered. He has over a million dollars in property and securities, so it's his money. Now what in hell does he gain by faking a kidnapping and paying out a million dollars of his own money?"

"I have a notion," Masuto said, "but I don't know whether I'm right."

"Suppose you let us in on your notion."

"Let me find out whether it makes any sense, Captain. Then I'd like to talk to the lot of them at the Barton place, Ranier and McCarthy and the Angel and a lady by the name of Elaine Newman, and also the three servants. If any of them left the Barton house, I'd like you to get them back in there and have Sy sit on the place until I get there."

"And that's going to help you find out who killed Barton?"

"I know who killed Barton."

"What!"

Masuto spread his hands and shook his head. "Not your way. I have no evidence. I see some kind of a crazy jigsaw puzzle, and I don't know what it is or why it is. So don't ask me to name any names."

"Why the hell not?" Wainwright demanded angrily.

"Because I can't do it that way. You know me a long time. This is like a dark tunnel and I'm feeling my way through."

Wainwright stared at him for a long moment; then he nodded. "All right, Masao, I'll play it your way for the next twenty-four hours. Then I want the name."

"Fair enough."

"Now what time at Barton's?"

"It's five now. Suppose we say between seven and seven-thirty."

Masuto left Beckman with Wainwright, and from San Yisidro he drove to Woodruff Avenue in Westwood, where his cousin, Alan Toyada, lived with his wife and three children. Toyada, who had been chief research analyst at Merrill Lynch for a number of years, had resigned to teach economics at U.C.L.A. and to conduct his own investment business. Masuto hoped to find him at home, and his hope was rewarded. After a series of polite greetings to the wife and the three children, he sat down in Toyada's study and explained that he had a problem.

"Which is why you're here, of course. What has happened to us since we nisei have become Americans? We abandon all the old ways. Family counts for so little. Do you know how many months it is since we have seen Kati and your children?"

"Too many. One lives with so much nonsense that the important things go by the board."

"How is Kati?"

"Very well. She has joined a consciousness-raising group, all nisei women. I think I approve."

"Do you? You might remember that one of the great advantages of being nisei is that one usually has a nisei wife. When you salt the kettle too much, it's very easy to spoil the stew."

"Perhaps. But I think we should talk about women's rights another time. Right now I have a problem that I present to your superior knowledge."

"Oh? Possibly the Barton kidnapping?"

"How do you know about the kidnapping?"

"Caught it on the radio driving home. The Angel was returned and the Bartons are happily reunited."

"Not quite. Mike Barton is dead—murdered."

"My God! When did that happpen?"

"A few hours ago."

"Do you know how, why?"

"How—yes. Shot in the head. But why—" Masuto shook his head. "That's why I come to you."

"To tell you why Mike Barton was shot? I am overwhelmed, Masao. A simple investment counselor called upon to explain the evil that men do. Actually, I am very flattered."

"You are by no means a simple investment counselor. You know more about the curious mythology of money than anyone else I might go to. So please try to help me."

"How can I refuse?"

"Very well. I'll be as brief as possible. Angel Barton was kidnapped. The ransom was a million dollars. The ransom was paid and Angel was released unharmed. My guess is that whoever received the ransom payment murdered Mike Barton. But it is the kidnapping itself that puzzles me."

"More than the fact of a crime?"

"Much more. In the first place, I don't believe that there ever was a kidnapping. I am convinced that Barton and his wife arranged a false kidnapping. But why?"

"Did he borrow the money?"

"No. But even if he had, his price is a million and a half dollars a film. But he didn't borrow the money. Of course, since he had only a few hours this morning to put together the million dollars, he had to go to the banks for cash, and he was helped by his producer, his lawyer, and his business manager. But every dollar was backed by securities Barton owned. Which means that he arranged a kidnapping and paid a million dollars of his own money to himself—or at least so he planned."

"You're sure the kidnapping was fraudulent?" Toyada asked him.

"If not, I should put away my police credentials and spend my declining years pumping gasoline. It was not only faked but stupidly faked."

"And your problem is to understand why it should have taken place at all?"

"Exactly. You see, early this morning, when Barton rejected an intervention on the part of the police or the FBI, I began to suspect the validity of the kidnapping. Then, as events unfolded, my suspicions were confirmed. The only thing that makes no sense whatsoever is the reason for the charade."

"But, Masao, when you found Barton's body, did you also find the million dollars?"

"No."

"Ah, so!"

"Yes, very Japanese. Do you do it purposely?"

"A habit of my father's."

"You would have made a good policeman, but my disgraceful profession is enough for the family to endure. Of course the person who killed Barton had motives easily understood. He wanted a million dollars. And this person also knew about the kidnap plot, whether or not he was directly involved in it. But Barton—?"

"Masao, you are a victim of the fact that policemen are grossly underpaid. The explanation is really very simple."

"It is? I feel like a fool already."

"Nonsense. It is simply outside your province. Mike Barton earned well over a million dollars a year. This money is paid as wages, and it is taxed by the government at a rate of fifty percent. But he also had very substantial additional income, which is categorized by the government as unearned income, and which in Mike Barton's case would have been taxed at a rate of seventy percent. Now what this income is, I have no way of knowing, but it's a safe guess that it was substantial."

"What kind of income?"

"Dividends on security holdings. Rents from real estate. Possibly shares in profits of films, depending on how they might have been structured. Any number of sources for what the government calls unearned income. Now when an actor works in a film, regardless of how much he is paid, a substantial part of his wages is withheld, just as a part of your own wages is withheld for tax purposes. But to some extent he decides how much should be withheld, and if there is a difference in the government's favor, he makes it up on April fifteenth, the date for filing. If there is a difference in his favor, the government sends him a check. Of course, you are aware of this. But with unearned income and with the income of self-employed professionals who are paid by fee as independent contractors, there is no withholding. The responsibility for the payment of taxes rests with the individual, and he must anticipate his tax and pay it to the government in four installments. Now keeping that in mind, let's return to Mike Barton. We'll propose that he needed a large amount of money desperately and quickly. Why? Was he being blackmailed? I leave that to you. You say that the million dollars was collateralized by securities? Are you sure? Have you checked? The money was put up by his friends—have they seen the securities? And how much of the million was an overdraft granted by the bank? If he has one of those enormous Beverly Hills houses, that would be security enough for an overdraft. But what have you checked?"

"At this point, nothing," Masuto said unhappily. "I saw no reason to question his friends concerning the securities."

"So we don't know how much of that million was his, but we can accept the fact that a substantial part was. He would have to clean out his bank accounts. Anyway, he needs money quickly and desperately. What to do? He and whoever was in it with him concoct a plan. Fake a kidnapping. Pay out a million dollars in ransom, which he can claim was his own money, and then take a million-dollar deduction on his income tax. If the entire million is in the seventy percent bracket, he nets a cool seven hundred thousand dollars of clear profit—plus his original million. But even if it's all in the fifty percent bracket, he has a very neat half a million dollars in profit. Of course, since the bills would be recorded, he'd have to launder the money. But no difficulty there. He pays the ten percent fee. It's regular big business south of the border and in the Bahamas."

"And the treasury allows it?"

"Masao, when a child is kidnapped, people bankrupt themselves to pay the ransom, and most kidnappings are not faked. Internal Revenue is pretty damned heartless, but this is America, and you know how people's hearts go out to a kidnap victim."

"And it's more or less foolproof, isn't it?"

"Except for stupidity, which you tell me this is laced with. However, considering that he would have paid ten percent to the launderers, Mike Barton would be holding nine hundred thousand dollars in cash. That's a lot of cash. What would he have done with it?"

"That's the question, isn't it? When I know that, I'll have all the other answers."

"How's that?"

"Just a guess that whoever killed Mike Barton did it for the money. I find the money, I find a killer—or killers."

5

The House on the Hill

North of Sunset Boulevard, in Beverly Hills, the land rolls up to the Santa Monica Mountains. The gentle slopes and hillocks are cut by several canyons, and the real estate in this area constitutes one of the most expensive residential neighborhoods in the entire country. The Barton home was on a hilltop just high enough to look out over the Beverly Hills Hotel, a Spanish colonial house on an acre of ground.

It was dark when Masuto pulled into the driveway, and four cars were already standing in the parking area. Beckman was waiting outside the front door, talking to a uniformed Beverly Hills cop, and he greeted Masuto with relief. "You got a houseful of angry citizens," he told Masuto, "especially McCarthy and Ranier, who insist that we got no right whatsoever to keep them here."

"We haven't. Why do they stay?"

"They tell it that the only reason they're here is to protect the rights of the Angel and to keep her from being bullied by the cops."

"Why do they think we'd bully her?" Masuto wondered.

"Because when they asked Wainwright whether they were

suspects, he said that he had to take the position that every-one who knew about the kidnapping was to some degree sus-pect. He said it more diplomatically, but McCarthy blew his top anyway. Barton's secretary—her name's Elaine Newman—went to pieces when she heard about the murder."

"Oh? And how did Mrs. Barton take it?"

"I don't know. She's been in her room since she got back. The doctor's been here to see her."

"What doctor?"

"Their family doctor, name of Haddam. He's gone now."

"And what about the FBI?"

"That kid, Frank Keller, was here. He nosed around and asked a few questions. Didn't seem to know what the hell he was doing."

"And the captain?"

"The captain went home to have dinner. McCarthy told him that any harassment of Angel Barton would result in an action, and that he'd sue the hell out of the city, and you know how the captain reacts when one of the wealthy citizens threatens to sue the city. He says that you can handle it, be-cause since you know all about who murdered Barton, you can go easy on everyone else. What about it, Masao? Do you know?"

"Sort of."

"What the devil does 'sort of' mean?"

"I know and I don't know."

"Sure. That clears it all up."

Beckman led the way into the house. "What about the press?" Masuto asked him.

"They were here, also the TV guys. Wainwright and McCarthy spoke to them. I told Frank, the officer at the door, not to let anyone in, except first he talks to you."

Masuto was studying the house thoughtfully. Earlier in the day he had seen it only from the outside. Inside, it displayed the slightly insane baronial overbuilding of a film star's house of the nineteen thirties—tile floor, huge center staircase, stained glass windows, light fixtures like chateau lanterns, ma-

hogany doors and trim and white plaster between heavy
wooden beams.

"They're in the living room—or were—over there." He nodded at an archway.

Masuto went down two steps, through the archway, and
opened a heavy door. The living room was at least forty feet
long, with a high, beamed ceiling, an overstuffed couch, some
easy chairs, and an enormous fireplace with a box large
enough to take five-foot logs. No fire burned there now. The
three people in the room were almost lost in its immensity—
McCarthy talking on the telephone, Ranier at a long deal
table with papers spread in front of him, and in one of the
big, overstuffed chairs, her legs drawn up under her, her eyes
staring sightlessly into space, a very pretty, slender young
woman who, Masuto surmised, was Elaine Newman. She had
dark hair and dark eyes and wore almost no makeup, and her
face had a chiseled quality that Masuto responded to immediately. After he and Beckman had entered the room and stood
just inside the door for a long moment, the girl turned to look
at him, but without curiosity. Ranier glanced up from his
papers and McCarthy finished his phone conversation.

"We met this morning," Masuto said. "I'm Detective Sergeant Masuto."

"Yes." McCarthy nodded. "I suggest you get on with your
inquisition and let us get out of here. I already informed
Wainwright that you have no damned right even to suggest
that we stay and be questioned."

"Only for you to help us," Masuto replied gently, "as citizens and as friends of the murdered man."

"They weren't his friends," Elaine Newman said unex-
pectedly and tiredly. "Don't call them his friends."

"Shut up, Elaine!" Ranier snapped.

"Why? Are you going to kill me too, you blood-sucking son
of a bitch?"

Ranier leaped to his feet and came around the table. "I
won't stand for that! I don't have to stand for that! I don't
have to listen to that foul-mouthed cunt!"

Beckman interposed himself, blocking Ranier's advance. "Let's all of us just take it easy," he said. "Why don't you sit down, Mr. Ranier?"

For a moment or two Ranier faced up to Beckman's enormous bulk; then he retreated and dropped into a chair. Beckman turned to Elaine Newman and said, "Why don't we go inside for a little while, Miss Newman. Suppose we find the kitchen and make us some coffee. I can use some, and I guess you can too." He glanced at Masuto, who nodded, and then he helped the girl out of her chair and led her to the door. "Can I go home?" she asked Masuto plaintively.

"In a little while. After we've talked. Go along with Detective Beckman and try to relax."

After Beckman and the girl had left the room, Ranier turned to Masuto and told him angrily, "I resent this. I resent having to stand here and be accused of murder by that little bitch."

"Bill, Bill," McCarthy said, "no one is accusing you of murder. Elaine is just shooting off her grief, and it's a relief to have some grief around here. Anyway"—he turned to Masuto —"Bill doesn't have enough guts to kill anyone."

"Thank you," Ranier said sourly.

"And Mike was his meal ticket. Who kills the goose that lays the five percent?"

"He was your meal ticket too!" Ranier shouted. "Talk about bloodsuckers—you soaked him with fees that were unreal."

"Which eliminates both of us as murder suspects. That ought to please you."

"That's enough of that," Masuto said sharply. "The fact of the matter is that Mike Barton is dead and someone killed him, and I have to make some sense out of this. All this talk of suspects is meaningless. We have no suspects. We have every reason to believe that Mr. Barton was killed for the million dollars of ransom money. Why whoever received the ransom found it necessary to kill him, we don't know. I'm hoping that one of you gentlemen can enlighten me."

"Have you spoken to Angel?" McCarthy asked. "She saw the kidnappers."

"You spoke to her?"

"We both spoke to her," Ranier said, "but she wouldn't talk about it—"

"She couldn't," McCarthy interposed.

"Then she couldn't. The doctor said she was in shock. Then when she heard about Mike's death, she went to pieces completely."

"Where is she now?"

"In her room."

"We have reason to believe," Masuto said, "that the person who killed Mr. Barton was known to him, perhaps a good friend."

"Mike had lots of friends."

"And no friends," McCarthy put in. "You have friends when you earn less than two hundred thousand a year. Above that, you have appendages. When you're a star, you have the star-fuckers, and the woods are full of them."

"Were you his friend?" Masuto asked gently.

"I'm going to ignore the insinuation. I was his lawyer. Bill here was his business agent."

"Yes, of course." Masuto studied them thoughtfully. "Mr. Barton, it appears, was killed some time between twelve-thirty and one o'clock. Without any insinuations, believe me, I must ask you gentlemen where each of you were at that time?"

"Right here," Ranier replied.

"Well," McCarthy said, "you did run back to your office."

"Later. Much later."

"Come on, Bill, it was not much later."

"What in hell are you trying to do?" Ranier demanded angrily. "Set me up?"

"I'm not setting you up. For Christ's sake, what are you so jumpy about? No one's accusing you of killing Mike. You're the last person in the world who had any reason to kill him. But the plain truth of the matter is that Mike got the ransom call at twelve noon on the button, and he bombed out of here with the money two minutes later. You left about ten minutes after that, and it was half-past one when you came back."

"I drove straight to my office."

"And where is your office?" Masuto asked.

"On Camden. My secretary keeps a log. She logs me in and she logs me out. She can bear witness to that. I had some work that had to be attended to. I didn't stay to finish it. I brought it back here with me."

"And when did you get back here?"

"It was about one-forty-five, I think. Lena Jones—she's the maid—she let me in."

"And while he was gone, for an hour and forty-five minutes, where were you, Mr. McCarthy?"

"You know you have no damned right to ask me any questions."

"I know that. You don't have to answer."

"I was right here, in this room. I made some phone calls, but I was right here."

"Alone?"

"Yes, alone. But Mrs. Holtz brought me a sandwich and coffee."

"When was that?"

McCarthy shrugged.

"You know damn well when it was," Ranier said. "You were eating the sandwich when I got back. You offered me the other one. I didn't even take time for lunch," he told Masuto.

"So what? I never left this room. Right now I would like to leave it. I've been cooped up here all day."

"You are both free to leave whenever you wish," Masuto said.

"If you're going to subject the Angel to questioning, I think I'll stay," McCarthy told him. "I'm her attorney."

"As you wish. And if you think of anything more you would like to tell me, I'll be in the kitchen."

"I'll take you there," Ranier said.

"I'm sure I can find the kitchen, and I would like to talk with Miss Newman privately."

"Can he do that?" Ranier demanded of McCarthy.

"Why not? I'm not her attorney and you're not her business manager."

"You know what she's going to say."

"I have no idea," Masuto said. He walked out of the room and through the hallway into what was apparently a butler's pantry. A sallow-faced man in his sixties sat there, reading a copy of *Sports Illustrated,* and he looked at Masuto inquiringly but without speaking.

"Sergeant Masuto, Beverly Hills police."

"I'm Kelly, the chauffeur."

"You live here?"

"Over the garage."

"I'd like you to stay in the house tonight. I want to talk to you later."

"Where would I go?"

Masuto went past him and opened a swinging door into the kitchen. It was an old-fashioned kitchen in size, better than twenty feet square, and recently modernized into the glittering perfection that most Beverly Hills homes required of their kitchens—but with the color scheme, perfection fled. The floors were yellow tile. The refrigerator, stove, and sink were finished in pink, and the walls in tile of mauve and tan. In the center of the room, at a large butcher-block worktable, Beckman sat with three women: the secretary, Elaine Newman; a stout, middle-aged woman whom he introduced as Mrs. Holtz, the cook; and a thin black girl who dabbed at her swollen eyes and who was introduced as Lena Jones, the parlormaid. Beckman himself was finishing a plate of stew and the last of a large mug of beer, and imagining she saw a look of disapproval on Masuto's face, Mrs. Holtz said, "Let him eat. Better the food shouldn't go to waste. Nobody has any appetite today."

"You hungry, Masao?" Beckman asked him.

He shook his head, thinking nevertheless that it was past his dinnertime and that he'd hardly get home much before mid-night.

Mrs. Holtz pressed him, and Masuto relented to the extent of a cup of coffee and a slice of pie. Then he asked the maid and the cook to wait in the dining room, telling them that he would like to talk to them later. When they had gone, he said to Beckman, "Get the chauffeur's full name and phone into L.A.P.D. See if they have any priors on him."

"His name is Joseph. Joseph Kelly," Elaine said. "He has a record, if that's what you're looking for. But he wouldn't kill Mike. Mike's the only one who's ever been decent to him. He was just a drifter without a hope in the world when Mike picked him up and gave him a job."

Masuto nodded at Beckman, who left the room. Sitting opposite the girl, he studied her thoughtfully.

"You're a nisei?"

"Yes."

"And you're the cop assigned to this case?"

"Yes."

"That means you have to find out who killed Mike."

"I hope to."

"Well, it's no big deal. I know who killed Mike."

"Oh? Who?"

"The Angel." She said it with loathing.

"Inside, you suggested that Ranier killed Mr. Barton."

"Maybe he did."

"Both of them?"

"They're both worthless bloodsuckers."

"You hate people."

"Some people. But I loved Mike. I was the only one around him who did, aside from Mrs. Holtz and Lena and Joe Kelly. All the rest"—her voice sank to a whimper—"oh, my God, it's like killing a kid, like killing a little boy. Why? Why did they do it?"

Masuto waited until she had regained control of herself, and then he asked her, "What about Joe and Della Goldberg? Did they love Mike?"

"I guess so. But after he married Angel—"

"The relationship cooled?"

"Yes."

"How long have you worked for Mike Barton?"

"Two years. Since right after he married Angel."

"What did your work consist of?"

"His correspondence. Also, he always wanted to write a book. All the stars do. They have this guilt thing about being where they are, and mostly they can't justify to themselves why they are where they are, and they feel that writing a book about themselves will be a way out. Poor Mike. He tried, but it was all too complicated."

"He dictated to you?"

"Yes. But we didn't get very far on the book. Twenty or thirty pages."

"I would like to read it, if you would allow me."

"Sure. Sure, why not?"

"Why do you hate Mrs. Barton?"

"The Angel? Because she's a phony. Because she's a mean, heartless bitch and because she gave Mike nothing but misery."

"Why didn't he divorce her?"

She thought about this for a while, and then she shook her head. "I don't know."

"Perhaps he loved her, the kind of love that demands nothing in return."

"Bullshit!" she said angrily. "My heart isn't broken because I lost a job. Mike has been my lover since almost the first day I was here. Are you going to tell me he loved that cold bitch?"

"I'm telling you nothing, only asking."

"I don't know why I'm talking to you at all."

"Because we both want to find out who killed Mike Barton, and I must ask questions which will disturb you. I ask you again, why didn't he divorce her?"

"He would never tell me. She had something on him."

"What?"

"I just don't know."

"Guess. You must have turned this over in your mind a thousand times."

"Ten thousand times."

"You say he didn't love her, yet he was willing to pay a million dollars ransom."

"Come on, Sergeant."

"What does that mean?"

"That whole kidnapping was a fraud. That little louse Ranier designed the whole thing."

"Why?"

"I don't know why. But I do know this, that if it were a real kidnapping, Mike wouldn't have given twenty cents to get her back. Oh, he might have had to make a public display of some kind, but keep the cops out, keep the FBI out? No way. I can see how Mike might have paid the kidnappers a million dollars to keep her—but to get her back? You've got to be kidding."

At this point Beckman came into the kitchen and said, "Masao, we got company. Della Goldberg is here with her husband, Joe, and Netty Cooper, and Roy Hennesy, the congressman from out in Malibu. They all claim to be dear friends of the deceased, so I put them in the living room."

"Dear friends," Elaine said bitterly.

"There are also a lot of media characters and Gloria Adams from the *Times*, and I guess I owe her."

"Keep them out—no reporters. You don't owe her that much. Let them go over to the station house and get it from our P.R."

"What P.R.? We don't have any P.R."

"Mac Bendix—he always knows what's going on, and he'll pump the captain and keep them up-to-date. But no reporters in the house. Also, if you can, keep the maid and chauffeur apart from the guests."

"Mrs. Holtz wants to make coffee. She says if you have guests, you got to feed them. The black kid is serving drinks. I don't know how I can chase her out."

"All right, let it go. What about McCarthy and Ranier?"

"They're still here, hanging in."

"I got a feeling they're all going to hang in. Do me a favor, Sy. Call Kati and tell her I'm here open end. I don't know when we'll get home."

Elaine Newman was staring at Masuto with interest. It was the first moment that some of the pain had left her face. As Beckman left, she said softly, "You know what you're doing, don't you?"

"I like to think so. I'm not sure."

"How come a man like you is a small-town cop?"

"We can talk about that some other time, and Beverly Hills is not any small town. Right now we come back to Ranier. Why are you so sure he engineered the kidnapping?"

"Because poor Mike didn't have enough brains to work it out, and the Angel has plenty of viciousness but not too many smarts."

"Why do you think Ranier planned it? Mind you, I neither agree nor disagree. I just want to know why you think so."

"Yes, I've been thinking. I got here about ten. I was here when you pulled that silly gardener charade—saw you through the window. Mike was in a black mood, not worried, not grief-stricken over the Angel, just mean and angry because he had been talked into doing something he didn't want to do. Usually he's gentle as a lamb. Or was. My God."

"Easy," Masuto said. "Try to relax. This has been very hard, but you're young and your whole life is ahead of you."

"You ever been in love, Sergeant?"

"Yes."

"Then don't tell me my whole life is ahead of me. I'm all right now. I was telling you about Mike's mood. I tried to talk to him, but that was no good. He wouldn't talk. I think I lost my temper and said something about if the kidnapping was real, why didn't he bring in the cops and the FBI? Then he told me to get out of the room. Ranier was there, and the way he looked at me, he could have killed me right then and there."

"You still haven't told me why you think Ranier planned
it?"

"He was Mike's business agent. You work in Beverly Hills,
so you know what a business agent is. He takes five percent of
everything Mike earned, and do you know what Mike earned?
It's only November now, and already Mike earned over three
million dollars. It sounds like a lot, doesn't it? It sounds like
enough to run a small country. But look what happens to it.
First of all, Ranier takes his five percent off the top. Then
McCarthy takes another ten percent off the top as Mike's
agent—my God, what's wrong with me? I keep talking about
him as if he were alive."

"I thought McCarthy was Mike's lawyer?"

"He is. But he also acts as his agent. That's common
enough. A lot of lawyers do it. He draws up the contracts with
Joe Goldberg and takes his ten percent for that. Then again,
as when Mike was sued by Bert Bailey, his stunt man,
McCarthy defended the suit. His fee for that was seventy
thousand dollars. Then the feds step in with their income tax,
and every bum in town with his hand stretched out, and
Mike's family back East, and Mike never said no to anyone.
I'm not saying that Mike doesn't need a business agent. He
could no more handle that kind of money than a five-year-old.
But Ranier is a crook, and I bet that when it comes to probat-
ing Mike's will, you'll find that he doesn't have twenty cents.
Ranier's taken care of that. That's why Ranier rigged the kidnapping and he and Angel murdered Mike."

"Tell me about Angel."

"You don't believe me."

"I believe that you have passionate feelings," Masuto said.
"I can't afford to have passionate feelings. I'm a policeman. I
need proof, evidence."

"Haven't I given you enough evidence?"

"Not evidence, Miss Newman. Opinions. And I respect your
opinions. I need your opinions."

"You're the strangest cop I ever met."

"Perhaps you've met very few. You said Mr. Barton didn't love Angel. Was there ever a time when he did love her?"

"I suppose when he married her."

"You suppose? Didn't he ever talk about it?"

"No! You keep asking me these questions. I'm sick. My whole world has gone down the drain, and you keep asking me about that bitch who killed him."

"Because I must. How did she feel about him?"

"Indifferent. What shall I say? They had separate rooms. Sure they appeared together at parties now and then. That was P.R. Otherwise she went her own way and Mike couldn't have cared less."

"What was her own way?"

"I don't know. No one knows. She has that little voice and that phony beatific smile, and it takes the whole world in."

"Was she having an affair with Ranier?"

"I don't know."

"Do you know where she came from?"

"France. Mike told me that once. It's all he ever told me about her. He wouldn't talk about her."

"But you say Mr. Barton loved you."

"Yes, yes, yes, damn you!"

"Then you must have discussed a future. That's the way people are, people like yourself, people with strong feelings."

"Yes, we discussed it. It was someday, always someday. When he no longer had to be a star," she added. Her eyes were filmed with tears. "Being a star. What a beautiful fate! Take a sweet, decent dumb kid from Brooklyn and turn him into a symbol for a nation of lunatics. I'll tell you what he said to me, Mr. Detective, and then you can make something out of it with your smart-ass, slant-eyed know-how!" Her anger poured out at the whole world and at Masuto, because he sat facing her. "He said he'd divorce that bitch just as soon as he could afford to face the world as a clown, as a ridiculous joke."

"A clown?"

"Yes. You heard me. A clown!"

"Miss Newman," Masuto said gently, "I can understand your feelings, but nothing is helped by venting your anger at me. We both want the same thing—to find out who killed Mike Barton."

"I told you who killed Mike."

"Then let's say we want to prove it, and to do that, you have to help me. Will you?"

For a long moment she hesitated; then she nodded. "I'll try."

"Good. Now a moment ago you said that Mike Barton felt he would have to face the world as a clown. You're sure that's the word he used?"

"Yes, clown."

"And a ridiculous joke?"

"That's what he said. A clown. A ridiculous joke."

"But why?" Masuto insisted. "Why those words? He could have said a fool, a turkey, a sucker, a shmuck—those are words used by a man out here who feels he has been taken to the cleaners by a woman. They're like code words. But a clown?"

"What difference does that make?"

"I think it makes a difference. Perhaps we'll talk about it again. You're upset, Miss Newman. Let me help you a little."

"How can you help me?" she demanded.

"Let me try. Empty your mind. Try to think of nothing at all. Just be here. We'll go on with this discussion, but if you can, simply hear my questions and give me answers, but don't evoke any images beyond that. Will you try?"

"It sounds crazy, but I'll try. I'll try anything. Otherwise I'll just go out of my mind."

6

The Returned Angel

"If you don't mind," Masuto said to Elaine Newman, "I'd like you to remain in the house for a while. That's not a police order or even a demand. It's just that you know a great deal about what went on here, and I'd feel comfortable if you were here."

"I can stay," she agreed listlessly. "There's a room upstairs that I use when I work late—or when Mike wanted me to stay over. Angel didn't object. I'd like to lie down for a while and see whether I can think my life into some kind of order."

"Does the door lock?"

"Yes." She looked at him curiously.

"Lock it." And as she got up, "One more thing, Miss Newman, tell me about the house."

"This house?"

"Yes. How many rooms, where they are—that sort of thing."

"Sure. There are five bedrooms upstairs, the master bedroom, which is Angel's, another bedroom which was Mike's—they've been in separate rooms since I came here to work—the room I use when I stay over, and two guest rooms. Behind the kitchen, through that door"—she pointed—"two servants' rooms. That's where Mrs. Holtz and Jonesey stay."

"Jonesey?"

"The black kid, Lena Jones. Joe Kelly sleeps in a little apartment over the garage. Through that door"—she pointed again—"the butler's pantry. No butler, just the pantry, and that door at the other end of the kitchen leads to the breakfast room. From the pantry one swinging door leads into the dining room, and the other opens into the hallway. You remember the way you came in with the big staircase facing you and the living room on your right. On the left there's the dining room, and at the front of the house, in front of the dining room, there's a library or den or whatever, and that's where I worked and took care of Mike's correspondence."

Beckman and Mrs. Holtz came into the kitchen while Elaine was speaking. "She insists," Beckman said.

"Because," Mrs. Holtz said, "it's after eight o'clock already, and some of these people eat no dinner. I don't have people in my house, I should let them starve."

"One more thing," Elaine said. "There's a game room with a pool table in the basement."

"You tell them," Mrs. Holtz said to Elaine. "Did Mr. Barton ever let anybody go hungry?"

"No, he fed the hungry."

"Where's Mrs. Barton?" Masuto asked Beckman.

"In her room. The doctor gave her a sedative and said she was to be left alone until he returned tomorrow."

"Crap! That's a load of crap!" Elaine exclaimed. "That lousy quack can't tell the living from the dead. I say she's up there in her room drinking champagne and eating caviar and celebrating."

"We'll see," Masuto said quietly, watching Mrs. Holtz, who had listened in silence to Elaine's outburst. "Right now, Sy, take Miss Newman here up to her room." When they had left the kitchen, he asked Mrs. Holtz, "Do you like Mrs. Barton?"

Her face stiffened. "I don't talk about the dead."

"Mr. Barton's dead, not his wife."

"To me, she's dead."

He went into the living room then. It was occupied by Netty Cooper, Congressman Hennesy, Della Goldberg, and her husband, Joe.

"Did Mr. McCarthy and Mr. Ranier leave?" Masuto asked them.

"Downstairs playing pool," Netty Cooper informed him.

"Yeah," Joe Goldberg said, "such is respect for the dead. Who are you?"

"The policeman I told you about," his wife said. "He is Detective Sergeant Masuto." Her eyes were red from weeping, and her voice trembled as she spoke. She fought inwardly to remain calm. "Where is Elaine? I want to see Elaine."

"I sent her up to her room," Masuto said. He went to the archway that led to the foyer and called Beckman. When Beckman appeared, he said to him out of the hearing of the others, "Take Mrs. Goldberg upstairs to Miss Newman's room. Make sure she locks the door again." And to Mrs. Goldberg, "If you go with Detective Beckman, he'll take you to Miss Newman."

After Della Goldberg left the room with Beckman, Hennesy asked Masuto whether he was new in the Beverly Hills police force.

"No, Mr. Hennesy, I'm not new to the force."

"Then you know that we don't browbeat people in Beverly Hills. We don't push them around."

"Yes, thank you for reminding me of that."

"Now, if you don't mind, we'll leave."

"Oh?"

"We're not leaving the house. Not yet. With cops all over the place, Angel needs someone to protect her. When you go, we'll go."

"Yes, of course. But before you go, might I ask you where you were at twelve-thirty today?"

"You know where I was, Sergeant. I was sitting on Mrs. Cooper's terrace out at Malibu, where you met me."

"That was considerably past twelve-thirty."

"That was considerably past the time I got there."

"How long was he there?" Masuto asked Mrs. Cooper.

"This is insufferable!" Hennesy said. "What in hell right do you have to stand there and question us?"

"The same right you have to refuse to answer," Masuto said, smiling.

"You're goddamn pleased with yourself, aren't you, taking over this house and pushing heartbroken people around."

"Oh, don't make such a fuss, Roy," Mrs. Cooper said. "I'm delighted to answer this Oriental gentleman's question. Do you know, Mr.—"

"Sergeant Masuto," he said politely.

"Do you know, Sergeant Masuto, one of the most unpleasant things a hostess can do is to look at her watch while guests are present. It's a crude signal that she wants them to leave. I wouldn't dream of doing it. So if the congressman says he was on my terrace at twelve-thirty, why he was. That's all there is to it." With that she took Hennesy's arm and they walked out of the living room.

"They're a cute pair, Officer," Joe Goldberg said. "They are that, a very cute pair." He was a short, fat man, bald, with a pair of sharp eyes hidden under shaggy brows. He took out a cigar now, offering another to Masuto, who shook his head. He clipped the end of the cigar and lit it, took a sip of the drink on the table next to his chair, and then puffed deeply and with satisfaction. "Lousy ticker," he said, "overweight, smoke too much, and here I am and poor Mike's dead. It's a stinking, fucked-up world, Officer, but I'm sure you know that."

"It has occurred to me. Tell me, was Mr. Barton on a picture when this happened today?"

"My latest. Half filmed, and it goes into the cutting room trash can. Five million dollars down the drain."

"But surely you were insured?"

"Yeah, insured. But that's not the game, is it? It takes a year to set up a film before the cameras begin to grind, and that year isn't insured. I lost my star and, like Della says, we lost a son too. Poor Mike—poor dumb bastard."

"Who do you think killed him?" Masuto asked casually, dropping into a chair facing the producer.

"Come on, come on, since when does a cop ask you that? This is my first murder, Sergeant—Masuto, isn't it? You're a nisei, if I'm not mistaken?"

Masuto nodded.

"I think I've seen your name in the papers. You're a pretty smart cop. The Japanese are damn smart, too smart for the rest of us, I'm afraid."

"I'm just a policeman, and you produce motion pictures," Masuto reminded him.

"I'm not sure that my job takes more brains than yours, and certainly a lot less guts. No, I have no idea who killed Mike, but I could name a lot of people who have a damn good reason for killing him, and they're all in this house—his friends, horseshit, pure, unadulterated horseshit."

"Please go on, Mr. Goldberg. You intrigue me."

"Start with McCarthy. He and Mike got into an argument at the Bistro two weeks ago, and Mike hit him across the face with his open hand. I don't know what the fight was about, but they tell me Jack just took it and stalked away. I don't know whether that's a reason for murder, but I suspect that McCarthy hates his guts."

"Still he rallied around this morning when the kidnapping took place."

"Ah, money talks. Mike is his best client. As for Bill Ranier, I've been pressing Mike to dump him. Ranier's a crook, and a business agent who's a crook is something no one needs. Ranier knows Mike was about ready to part company with him. As for that little tart they call Angel, she's not shedding any tears over Mike's death. I imagine it was the answer to her prayers."

"And the congressman and Mrs. Cooper?"

"She's a silly woman, and you can drop her off the list. Hennesy is another matter. Shady, and once very close to being indicted for bribe-taking. They say he's mad about the Angel, but that's a thin rumor. The Angel is shacked up with someone, but who it is I don't know. But then a million dollars talks pretty damn loud, doesn't it?"

"So they say. And yourself, Mr. Goldberg?"

"Sure." Goldberg nodded, staring at his cigar ash. "Don't leave me out. I could have killed Mike ten times over—for being a horse's ass, for marrying that bitch, for not divorcing her, for letting Ranier rob him blind—ah, what the hell difference does it make now?"

"Why didn't he divorce her?"

"You know, there was a time when Della and me, we were like a mother and father to Mike. He would invite himself to dinner two, three times a week. He would bring his dates for our approval. He would beg Della to read his lines with him. Oh, I don't claim it was all disinterested affection for the kid. I made him a star and he was worth his weight in gold to me. But beyond that, we were both crazy about him—until—" He stared at Masuto. "You want to listen to all this garbage?"

"Yes, I do."

"Okay. Until he met the Angel. She was dealing twenty-one in Vegas. That was two—two and a half years ago. Mike was a hot gambler, but the stories about him losing two or three hundred thousand in a session are pure bullshit. When Mike went to Vegas, he'd take a couple of thousand with him and when it was gone, he was finished. Well, as I said, he meets this Angel, it's love at first sight, and she quits her job which she had only a few days. They're married right there in Vegas and she comes back with him, and for a week or so Mike is happy as a clam, and then it's over."

"Same question, Mr. Goldberg. Why didn't he divorce her?"

"Did you ask Ellie Newman? She's a nice kid. She and Mike were in love with each other."

"I asked her. She claimed she didn't know, and the closest she ever came to an answer from Mr. Barton was his belief that it would make him a clown, a joke in the eyes of the world. I guess he intimated that it would end his film career."

"Poor dumb kid. Well, that's more of a reason than I ever got. She had something on him. I don't know what it could be—" He shook his head hopelessly.

"And the kidnapping this morning. Did you buy it, Mr. Goldberg?"

"What do you mean, did I buy it?"

"I mean," Masuto said slowly, choosing his words carefully, "did you feel that it was a real kidnapping or a faked kidnapping?"

"How the hell should I know? Sure I knew that Mike wouldn't have given twenty cents to get her back, but the public wouldn't buy that, and if Mike had refused to pay the ransom for his wife's life, that would wash him out as a working star. We talked about that, and I agreed that he should pay it."

"Did you also agree that he should keep the police and the FBI out of it?"

"Did he? I didn't know that." He shook his head worriedly. "Why would he do that? He had to pay the ransom, but I'd think he'd have the cops in there every step of the way." He stared at the curl of smoke rising from his cigar. "Sergeant?"

"Yes?"

"How long do we have to stay here?"

"You don't have to stay here at all. You can leave whenever you wish."

"Well, I'll wait until my wife finishes talking to Ellie."

Masuto nodded and left the room. Beckman was in the hall outside talking into a telephone. Masuto waited. Beckman put down the telephone.

"Where are they?"

"Downstairs in the game room."

"Any of them leave?"

Beckman shook his head. "It's like they're all watching each other. Mrs. Goldberg is still upstairs with Newman. Angel's still in her room."

"And Kelly?"

"He's in the kitchen with Mrs. Holtz. The black kid is

downstairs. They keep her running for drinks. By the way, Doc Baxter called. It was a twenty-two short, just as we thought, and he still fixes the time of death between twelve-thirty and one. One more thing—" Beckman paused, relishing the moment. "Wainwright had a couple of cops canvassing the houses on San Yisidro. They found a kid who saw a yellow two-seat Mercedes drive by at about twelve-thirty or so. He remembered it because it's his dream car, and he never saw it before."

"Did he notice who was driving, a man or a woman?"

"No. He was at an upstairs window, being sick with the flu, so he never saw who was driving."

Masuto thought about it for a while, and then he said to Beckman, "Sy, I want to talk to Angel Barton, and I don't want anyone else talking to her first. So go upstairs and wait for me outside her room. No one goes in—but no one. And if she wants to leave, just delay her. I won't be more than ten minutes."

"This Dr. Haddam said—"

"I don't give a damn what Dr. Haddam said."

"Okay, okay, Masao. What's eating you?"

Masuto laughed and shook his head. "I'm sorry, Sy. We live in an insane world."

"What else is new?"

"I try to suspend judgment. Sometimes that's almost impossible. What did you find out downtown about Joe Kelly?"

"He has a record, like Miss Newman said. Seven priors. In and out, he spent maybe twenty years in jail, all of it theft, grand larceny, petty larceny. He's a thief, that's all. He got out on parole eight years ago, and Mike Barton hired him. He's been clean ever since."

"All right. Go upstairs now. I'll join you in a few minutes."

Masuto went into the kitchen. Kelly and Mrs. Holtz sat at the kitchen table, each with a cup of tea. Mrs. Holtz was a woman of at least fifty, possibly even sixty years. She was crying, yet seemingly unaware of the tears rolling down her cheeks. Kelly sat watching her, his long, lined and battered face impassive. But that, Masuto realized, could be misleading. A man who had lived Kelly's life would be beyond the point of revealing emotions facially. Masuto felt the tragedy of his own aloofness, but it was a tragedy mankind shared, the tragedy of being fragmented, of each person being walled away from the suffering of others. There was little left for those two people. In all likelihood Kelly could never find another job.

Masuto pulled a chair up to the table, waving Mrs. Holtz back to her seat as she started to rise. "Don't get up, please."

"I'll get you a cup of tea, Sergeant. A piece of cake."

"No. No, thank you. Just a few questions."

"You might as well know about me," Kelly said. "I got a record."

"I know."

"I never slugged anyone and I never shot anyone. I was never busted for carrying a gun."

"I know that."

Mrs. Holtz evidently did not know it. She stared at Kelly in astonishment.

"And I never left this place today."

"Yes. Then you saw Mr. Barton leave with the ransom money?"

"I was washing a car in front of the garage when he pulled out. He had a big brown suitcase, and he put it on the front seat of the car next to him."

"What time was that?"

"Maybe ten, fifteen minutes past twelve, because after he pulled away I turned off the water and came into the kitchen here for my lunch."

"That was twenty minutes after twelve," Mrs. Holtz said. "I remember."

"Why do you remember the exact time?" Masuto asked her.

"Because inside, in the living room, Mr. McCarthy and Mr. Ranier was having terrible argument. Joe heard it too. He said, 'What do you think? Maybe they're hungry.' It was joke. I said, 'No, it's only twenty minutes after twelve.'"

"Did you hear what they were saying?"

"I don't listen. Maybe Joe?"

He shook his head.

"Mrs. Barton was kidnapped," Masuto said, "and in great danger. Yet you were able to joke about things."

Mrs. Holtz shrugged. "Is terrible not to care about someone, but she was never nice to us."

The telephone rang, and Masuto picked up the extension on the kitchen wall. It was Klappham, on night duty at the station house. "The captain left me this number, Masao," he said. "Bones down at L.A.P.D. called and left this message for you. They picked up the yellow Mercedes. It was parked on Fourth Street downtown. No damage. Mint condition and the key in the lock."

"Did they dust it?"

"I was just going to tell you, wiped clean."

Masuto hung up the telephone and turned back to Kelly. "Did you ever drive for Mrs. Barton?"

"Sometimes."

"Did you ever take her to meet anyone?"

"Maybe, but I don't know who she met."

"What does that mean?"

"Well, a lot of times, I drive her down to the Music Center. I drop her off and she'd tell me when to pick her up. Same thing out to Malibu, if she didn't want to bother to drive. We got that big Lincoln Continental chauffeur car, with a bar in it and a telephone and all that garbage, and I guess it made her feel pretty classy riding around in it. She didn't like my driving, but when you been busted as many times as I have, you drive careful, and when she was alone with me she could really let go. She could talk pretty damn dirty. Sometimes she'd cuss me out in French. I don't know the words, but from the way she spit it out I knew she was cussing me. She was always after Mr. Barton to dump me and hire someone else."

"Did you ever take her to meet a man—I mean did you ever actually see her with a man?"

"Once, when I had to pick her up at the County Museum, she was kissing someone."

"Who?"

"That's it. I was coming down Wilshire, maybe two, three blocks away. When I got to her, he was gone."

"Yes. Do you know whether either of the Bartons owned a gun?"

"Yes," Mrs. Holtz said. "Yes. She left it one day on her dressing table. No, not on it—inside. You know how the top comes up with a mirror. It was there, and Jonesey saw it. It scared her to death. Jonesey was cleaning the room, and she came running to me."

"Did you see the gun?"

Mrs. Holtz nodded.

"Can you describe it for me?"

"It was small, silver, very small. Like a toy gun. Like guns you see, but they're really cigarette lighters."

"Thank you. I'll talk to Miss Jones later. You've been very helpful."

Masuto went upstairs then and joined Beckman, who was waiting for him outside the door of Angel Barton's room. "Anything?" he asked Beckman.

"Quiet as a grave. Nobody in, nobody out. There's still reporters and TV characters outside, but Dempsy's held the line against them. You'd think the telephone would be ringing constantly, but the black kid they call Jonesey tells me that they have an unlisted number and they keep changing it. Still, you'd think a star would have loads of friends."

"You'd think so," Masuto said. He tapped at the door of Angel's room. "Where's Miss Newman and Mrs. Goldberg?"

"That room, down the hall," Beckman said, pointing.

Masuto knocked at the door again, waited a few seconds, and then turned the handle and opened the door. The room was pink and white—white carpet on the floor, pink walls, white bed, pink coverlet, two pink and white angels suspended by wire from the ceiling fleeting over the bed, mirrors on one whole wall, white baroque furniture, a pink and white chaise longue, and lying on it, half-reclining, Angel Barton in a pink robe over a white silk and lace nightgown. Her hair was a hairdresser's triumph—long, spun gold, and two wide, innocent blue eyes stared at them out of a Marilyn Monroe face.

The two men halted just inside the door, staring at Angel who returned their stare unblinking.

"Sy, close the door," Masuto whispered.

He closed the door and said, "Masao, what the hell goes on here?"

Masuto walked over to Angel Barton and picked up her arm. There was no pulse and the hand was cold.

"Is she dead, Masao?"

He pushed the lids down over the staring blue eyes. "Very dead, I think." On the floor next to the chaise longue there was an empty hypodermic needle. Beckman picked it up with his handkerchief.

"How long?" he asked Masuto.

Staring at Angel thoughtfully, Masuto said, "The hands are cold. Twenty minutes, half an hour." He was examining her arm. There was a single puncture mark. "What's the smell?" he asked Beckman, who was sniffing the air.

"Ether."

"I thought so. Go downstairs, Sy, and tell Dempsy that no one leaves the house. I've been stupid, and I don't want to go on being stupid. Then call the station and tell them to get another cop over here and to inform the captain. Then call Baxter and tell him we want him and an ambulance."

"He'll love that."

"We'll try to live with his displeasure."

Beckman was studying the hypodermic. "No prints."

"No, he wanted to get rid of it, so he wiped it and dropped it."

Beckman left the room. Masuto walked over to the dressing table and raised the lid. There was the gun Mrs. Holtz had spoken about. It was a small, expensive purse gun, twenty-two caliber and probably, Masuto guessed, of Swiss make. He took it out, hooking his pinky through the trigger guard and then brought it into the light of a lamp, studying it carefully. It bore a clear set of prints which, he was convinced, would match those of the dead Angel. He then wrapped it in his handkerchief and dropped it into his pocket.

He then walked over to the dead Angel and stared at her thoughtfully. She was indeed a very beautiful woman, even in death. He tried to analyze his own feelings. Had he been the cause of her death? Was his own failure to anticipate it to be condemned? Should he have known? There was something missing. He was not attempting to exonerate himself. There was simply something missing.

He bent over the dead woman now and raised one of the eyelids he had closed before, peering at the cold blue eye it revealed. Then he lowered the lid again. There were two doors at one side of the bedroom. Masuto went to them now. One led to a bathroom, where tile and sink and tub were in varying shades of pink. The other door opened on an enormous walk-in closet.

Masuto flicked on the closet light, staring at the racks of dresses, slacks, and evening gowns. One entire wall of the closet was devoted to a shoe rack, holding at least a hundred pairs of shoes and, at the bottom, four pairs of riding boots. He then went through the racks and finally found, not on the racks, but carefully folded on a shelf behind the dresses, six pairs of whipcord breeches. What this added up to, Masuto could not for the life of him imagine. Possibly nothing. Possibly she liked to ride. In the detective stories he read occasionally, everything pointed in a specific direction. But here were things most curious that pointed nowhere.

7

The Departed Angel

"You don't need me," Dr. Baxter said sourly. "I don't have to dance attendance on every corpse you clowns turn up. I was in the middle of my dinner—"

"It's ten o'clock," Wainwright said apologetically.

"Civilized people eat late, and if you think I'm going to spend all night doing an autopsy, you're crazy. I'll get at it in the morning."

"All we want to know," Wainwright begged him, "is why she died."

"Because her heart stopped. It causes death."

"Come on, Doc, be reasonable."

"Are you reasonable? What do you think they pay me to be medical examiner for this silly town of demented millionaires. All right, you want to know what she died of? I'll tell you what she didn't die of. She didn't die of an overdose of heroin, if that's what you're thinking. She's not a user."

"Was she murdered?"

"How the hell do I know whether she was murdered? I'm not a cop, and I can't read the minds of the dead. When I cut her up, I'll tell you what I find."

"You can take her away," Wainwright told the stretcher bearers. They left the bedroom with the body, Baxter stalking after them.

"He's a doll," Beckman observed. "He's just a sweet, good-natured doll."

Sweeney, glancing up from his search for fingerprints, blamed it on Baxter's profession. "You do that kind of work, it's got to show."

The photographer was still working his flashbulbs. "The body's gone," Wainwright said tiredly. "That's enough. Take what you got back to the station and develop it."

"I don't know how the word gets around. Maybe it's ESP," Beckman said. "But there's two TV crews outside and four or five reporters. Someone's got to talk to them."

"I'll talk to them. Just tell them to wait and be patient." Beckman left the bedroom. Wainwright slumped down on the chaise and said to Masuto, "What makes you so damn sure she was murdered?"

"It had to be. Only I didn't have enough sense to realize it."

"I don't know what in hell you're talking about, Masao, but I know one thing. This afternoon you told me you knew who killed Mike Barton. No more games. I want the name."

"All right. But it doesn't finish anything. Angel Barton killed her husband—but only in a legal sense. She was with a man, and the man pulled the trigger. Of course, she was part of it. They planned the thing together. And the stakes were high—one million dollars in cold cash, and if it worked, any-thing she was entitled to in his will." Masuto reached into his pocket and took out the gun he had wrapped in his handker-chief. "Here's the gun that killed Mike Barton."

Wainwright stared at it speechless. Sweeney came over, lifted the little pistol carefully by its trigger guard, and ex-amined it in the light of a lamp.

"As lovely a set of prints as I've ever seen."

"Where did you get it?" Wainwright demanded.

"Over there—in her dressing table. Where the killer had placed it after he finished with Angel. The prints are excellent. He put them on the gun after Angel was dead, pressing her fingers to it."

"And how did he kill her?"

"I don't think we'll ever know that. My guess is that he knocked her out with something, perhaps ether, and then he injected her vein with air. I don't know whether that can be proven in an autopsy. They may find traces of something in the syringe. He was desperate and in a hurry, and I guess he decided to make it look like suicide. It was a stupid, witless crime from the moment it started this morning."

"Yeah, when it's not stupid, we don't even know that a crime took place. I guess you're right about the gun, but we'll let Ballistics decide. You said this morning, you think the whole kidnap caper was a rigged job?"

"A kid's job. I think the husband, Mike Barton, was in on it, and then his Angel double-crossed him and brought someone else into it. Or maybe the whole thing started with the killer. I couldn't make any sense out of the kidnap thing until I spoke to a cousin of mine who's an expert on legal ways to cheat Internal Revenue, and he said that there would have been a big tax break for Barton."

"Except that from what I hear, neither Barton nor the Angel were smart enough to figure it out."

"Exactly. There's another small matter," Masuto said. "The killer is right here in this house."

"You're sure?"

"Very sure. No one came in when it was done, no one left."

"That's beautiful." Wainwright rose and began to pace the room. "Pink and white, pink and white, she must have really seen herself as some goddamn kind of angel. They don't want a cop for my job, they want a diplomat. Downstairs, we only got one of the most prominent lawyers in town, a top film producer, a hotshot business manager, and a congressman. Plus a chauffeur with a record long as my arm."

"Not to mention a number of women who are probably a lot smarter than the men."

"And a fed. That kid from the FBI pushed his way in and

started bugging me about what was his role in all this. I told him how the hell did I know what his role was? He's a goddamn idiot. He's got a notion that the Mafia is mixed up in it because he heard we found a syringe in here."

"Is he still here?"

"Prowling around downstairs. I can't throw him out. We've had too many run-ins with the feds."

"We'll both be very kind to him."

They had their opportunity almost immediately. As they went downstairs from the second floor of the Barton house, they saw Frank Keller waiting for them at the foot of the staircase, his pink-cheeked, snub-nosed face set in a grimace of determination. He was wearing a carefully pressed gray flannel suit, a white shirt, and a tie with brown and maroon stripes. Masuto, who wore an old brown tweed jacket over rumpled trousers and a tieless shirt, had once been asked by another FBI man whether he always dressed that way or only when in disguise.

"I've been trying to work out my role here," Keller said. "I don't want to push in like a bull in a china shop."

"That's very considerate of you," Masuto agreed.

"On the other hand, there's been a kidnapping, even though both the victim and the ransom payer are dead. You know, it's a national tragedy. I don't think anything quite like this ever happened before. You think of Mike Barton and you think of Robert Redford, Al Pacino, John Wayne—although I don't think it would have happened to John Wayne in just this manner."

"I guess not," Masuto agreed.

"Of course, the murders are a local matter, if murder is the correct term?"

"We think Angel Barton was murdered," Wainwright told him. "We won't know for certain until after the autopsy. We found a syringe and a puncture mark—which is all we know for sure."

"You could do one thing that would be very helpful," Masuto said.

"Be glad to."

"We can be pretty certain that if Mrs. Barton was murdered, someone here in the house at this moment killed her. And we can work up a background on every one of them except Mr. Hennesy."

"Congressman Hennesy?"

"That's right."

"But surely," Keller protested, "you can't suspect Congressman Hennesy of an act of murder."

"I have to. I have to suspect every one of them."

"We're not accusing him or anyone else," Wainwright explained, talking softly, since from their position at the foot of the stairs they could hear the chatter of voices from the living room. "Believe me, here in Beverly Hills, a thing like this is no picnic. One wrong move on our part and we could face a million-dollar lawsuit—and that fellow McCarthy in there is one of the sharpest lawyers in town. That's why we'd like you to get us a rundown on Hennesy. Your office must have everything there is to have on him."

"I'll try. I don't know what they'll say in Washington. Is he involved in the kidnapping?"

"I don't know," Masuto said.

"Does anything point in that direction?"

"If you wanted to point it, you could. He was at the same party Angel attended the night she was kidnapped, but when we talked to him about it this afternoon, he seemed to have forgotten that he left the party with her. He offered a lie as an alibi without being accused of anything. I don't know what it adds up to, but if you want to make a connection with the kidnapping for the people in Washington, there's enough there."

"All right. I'll do my best. But it won't be sooner than noon tomorrow."

"We understand."

"You don't mind if I stick around for a while?"

"Be our guest," Wainwright said generously, and then he led the way into the living room.

They were all there—McCarthy and Ranier and Joe Goldberg and his wife, and Congressman Hennesy and Mrs. Cooper and Elaine Newman—with Beckman leaning his huge figure against a grand piano and watching them with calculated indifference.

"You have no right to hold us here," McCarthy said immediately. "You know that, Captain Wainwright. From what I gather, you don't know what caused Angel Barton's death. This is Beverly Hills, and I find it outrageous that this oversized officer of yours"—he indicated Beckman—"should tell us that we are not to leave."

"If he told you that, he was mistaken," Wainwright said placatingly. "Of course you are free to leave whenever you wish. I only suggested that we would like to have a few words with you, that is with any of you who don't have to leave immediately. You were friends of the Bartons, and in that capacity you could be very helpful. But if you wish to leave, McCarthy, there's no reason why you shouldn't."

"For how long?"

Wainwright turned to Masuto. "Ten, fifteen minutes," Masuto told them. "Your assistance would be invaluable. But as the captain said, any of you who wish to leave now are free to do so."

No one moved. Hennesy said, "Since as a concerned citizen I am to be part of this charade, I'd like a drink."

Wainwright nodded at Lena Jones, who was hovering in the doorway. She came forward slowly.

"Take orders from all of them," Masuto told her. "Is Kelly still around?"

"He's in the pantry. He'll make the drinks."

"All right. Bring back the drinks, and then we're not to be disturbed."

While the people gathered in the living room were giving their orders for drinks, Beckman walked over to Masuto and whispered, "Any way to smell their hands, Masao?"

Masuto chuckled. "Want to try? Ether leaves an odor, but there's soap and perfume."

"Just a notion."

To Wainwright, Masuto said softly, "I want to tell them that Angel was murdered."

"Will it help?"

"I think so."

"Is it one of them?"

"Or Beckman or myself or one of the three servants. No one else was in the house."

"Go ahead and do what you got to do."

"I'll step on toes."

"There's no other way. The city manager will be in my office tomorrow morning yelling his head off. But he'll yell at me, not at you. So just take it with a grain of salt if I put you down and save face."

"I'm all understanding."

Jones returned now with the drinks, and when she had left the room, Masuto said to the assembled company, "I must begin by telling you that Angel Barton was murdered, and we have every reason to believe that she was murdered by the same person who killed her husband. I must add that the murderer is still in the house, since no one entered or left this house since at least an hour before the murder took place. That doesn't mean the murderer is in this room, not necessarily, since there are also three servants in the house. This information does not change what Captain Wainwright said before. There are no charges against any of you, and any one of you is free to leave when he or she pleases."

"And to be tagged as your mysterious killer!" Mrs. Cooper snorted.

"This whole procedure is outrageous," McCarthy said. "I challenge your statement that no one entered or left this house this evening. There are French doors, a kitchen door, a basement door—there are windows. How dare you come in here with your asinine conclusions and browbeat a group of people whose only sin is that they were the close friends of Mike and Angel Barton!"

"There'll be no browbeating, Sergeant!" Wainwright snapped.

"Terribly, terribly sorry," Masuto said. "Please forgive me if I gave any impression of browbeating. You may leave now, if you wish, Mr. McCarthy."

"I have clients here. I will not leave them without legal protection."

"Would anyone else like to leave?"

No one moved.

"Then I must tell you, as Mr. McCarthy certainly would have, that you have the right to ignore any questions I may ask you. I shall question each person in turn, and I would appreciate it if the others did not interfere. Except, of course, Mr. McCarthy, who will be duty-bound to advise his clients not to answer when he feels they should not answer."

"I'm not sure I want to answer any of your damned questions," Hennesy said.

"As you please, Congressman. I'll start with Mrs. Goldberg."

Beckman had moved behind them. He sat on the piano bench, his notebook out.

"Do you ride, Mrs. Goldberg? I mean horseback."

Della Goldberg observed him with interest, smiling slightly. "As a matter of fact, I do. I mean, I try. It's silly at my age, but most of the things one does out here are silly."

"Where do you ride?"

"In Malibu. My husband and I keep horses at the Grandview Corral."

"And you both ride?"

"We both try."

"Thank you. And you, Mr. McCarthy, do you ride?"

McCarthy stared at him, his face set.

"Of course he does," Mrs. Cooper said, "and I don't blame him for refusing to answer a stupid question like that. And I ride, if you intend to ask me that dumb question. At the same Grandview Corral."

"I ride occasionally," Ranier volunteered. "I don't know

why you want to know and I couldn't care less. At Crushanks, the Valley."

"And you, Mr. Hennesy?"

"I think I've had enough of your nonsense, Masuto. I didn't like you when I met you this afternoon, and I like you less now. The abuse of police power is one of the things I like least in this democracy of ours. To have a very mournful occasion like this turned into a circus is more than I can endure. I think I'll leave." He stood up. "Will you join me?" he asked Mrs. Cooper.

"As a matter of fact, I was thinking the same thing." She rose too.

"I'll go with you," McCarthy said, and to Ranier, "I'd advise you to do the same thing, Bill."

"I'll stay," Ranier decided.

McCarthy, Hennesy, and Mrs. Cooper left the room. Masuto heard the door slam as they departed from the house, and Wainwright took the moment to whisper to Masuto that he was going home. "It's your ballgame, Masao," he said. "I'm going to get to the city manager tonight, before McCarthy shits all over us. And be careful," he added, dropping his voice still further. "We got McCarthy and we got the congressman, and those are two mean bastards. So for God's sake, keep it cool and don't involve us in any lawsuits. And don't make any arrests. These people aren't going anywhere."

The Goldbergs, Miss Newman, and Ranier sat quietly, waiting. When Wainwright had left, Joe Goldberg said, "What now, Sergeant? I'll admit I am an appropriate candidate for murdering the Angel, if I had enough guts to murder anyone, which I haven't, but poor Mikey I would kill only for his stupidity, and no one kills because someone they love is stupid."

"Mikey wasn't so stupid," Della Goldberg protested. "He was trusting."

"Which, carried to the extremes he carried it to, was simply another form of stupidity."

"Will you two stop!" Miss Newman cried. "You just can't stand the fact that Mike decided he didn't need another mother and father. Calling him stupid because he loved people and trusted them!"

"I think you'd better go home, Miss Newman," Masuto said gently. "You've had a long, terrible day." And to Beckman, "Take her outside, Sy, and have a squad car drive her home."

"I have my car here," she muttered, the tears beginning.

"All right, if you wish. And please give Detective Beckman your address and phone number."

"Anything more?" Goldberg asked after the girl and Beckman had gone.

"Yes. Do you know whether Hennesy rides?"

"He rides," Ranier put in.

"What is this riding business?" Goldberg asked. "How does it fit in?"

"I'm not sure I know."

Beckman came in then and told Masuto that Kelly had asked whether he could go to his room. "He sleeps over the garage."

"Yes, he can go." And then to Ranier, "How do you know Hennesy rides?"

"I was once a guest out at Albermarle, near San Fernando. They told me he keeps a horse there."

"That would cost a bundle," Goldberg remarked. "Hennesy doesn't have a pot to pee in."

"Hennesy's on the take. When he needs money, he gets money. All right, I don't smell of roses. It takes one to know one."

"What kind of take?" Masuto asked.

"I can give you a list of what a congressman can do for you as long as your arm. He does it."

Keller, the FBI man, spoke up for the first time since he had entered the room and said, "That's a serious accusation, Mr. Ranier."

Ranier looked at Masuto hopelessly. "Is he kidding?"

"I think not. He's a federal officer."

"And you work in this town," Ranier said to Keller, "and you never heard that Roy Hennesy is a crook?"

"Come on, Bill," Goldberg said, "you don't call a man a crook until you can quote chapter and verse. Anyway, I've had enough of this whole thing. My wife and I would like to leave, Sergeant."

"If you wish, of course."

As he rose, he asked, "Are we still suspects?"

"Did you or your wife kill the Bartons?"

"You know damn well we didn't!"

Masuto shrugged. "At this point, I know so little."

The Goldbergs departed, leaving Masuto with Ranier and Keller. Ranier rose, took a few paces, leaned over the piano with his back to the two men, and then turned to Masuto and said, "I want to talk to you."

"Very well."

"Alone."

"All right." And to Keller, he said, "You might as well tie it up for the night, Mr. Keller. We've lost everyone except Mr. Ranier, and he wants privacy."

Keller was not to be dismissed so easily. "Those are very serious charges, Mr. Ranier, and directed against a congressman, they become even more serious. Unless you can back them up with hard evidence, they are certainly actionable."

"Screw him!" Ranier said angrily. "If Hennesy wants to sue me, let him sue me. I don't give a damn. If your goddamn Justice Department knew its ass from its elbow, you wouldn't have people like Hennesy making a career out of the take!"

"I don't think this ought to go any further tonight," Masuto told them. "We're all tired and upset. If you want to go into this with Mr. Ranier, I suggest you do it tomorrow."

Keller seemed ready to stand his ground. Then he nodded. "All right, I'll take it downtown, and then we'll see. Good night, Sergeant." He showed his displeasure by not even glancing at Ranier as he left.

"Stupid son of a bitch," Ranier said.

"You wanted to talk, Mr. Ranier."

Ranier dropped into a chair and put his face in his hands.

Tired, Masuto sat facing him. Masuto waited. He rarely urged anyone to speak; it was better to wait.

When Ranier looked up, his face was drained. It was the thin, parched face of a man who had run all his life without ever catching up with himself. "You got me pegged for Angel's murder," he said finally. "You got me pegged for Mike's murder."

"What makes you think so?" Masuto asked.

"Don't give me that soft Oriental shit, Masuto. I know who you are and how you work. I haven't lived in this town for twenty years without knowing which side is up. I know about you and how you work, and goddamnit, I won't go down for two killings."

"If you didn't do them . . ." Masuto shrugged.

"Look, I'm going to come clean with you. I don't know whether what I did was legal or illegal, but it wasn't murder. Whatever you may think, the truth is that I was trying to help Mike. I liked Mike."

Beckman came in now. "What about it, Masao? Should I take off?"

Masuto nodded, and Beckman left. Ranier was staring at his hands. "I liked Mike," he said softly, "but he was a damn idiot. Who else but an idiot would marry Angel? And I didn't steal from him. I made good investments, but it was real estate and the money was tied up. He owed half a million dollars in taxes, and he didn't have it. The money should have been paid in September, and here it is November. And why? Because he'd sneak off to Vegas and drop a hundred grand in one night. So I cooked up the kidnapping. That's right, it was my idea, a stupid idea, but I'm not the first one to go stupid. We had to borrow most of the money, but we could pay it back after we laundered it, and we'd make half a million and better out of the tax deduction. Mike and Angel agreed to go along with me, and now they're dead."

"Was any of the money yours?"

"About a hundred thousand dollars."

"Suppose you tell me exactly how you laid it out."

"Some of it you know. Angel made the fake entry out at Malibu, and then she drove her car to my place. She had the key, and she was there until twelve o'clock. Then she made the call to Mike, and after that she was supposed to drive downtown to Fourth Street, where Mike would pick her up. They'd leave the car there, and the story would be that after Mike had made the drop on San Yisidro, or claimed that he made the drop, he was instructed by the phony kidnappers to pick her up in Benedict Canyon, and then he was to bring her back here."

"Why drive to San Yisidro at all? Why didn't he go straight downtown and pick up his wife?"

"In case he was followed. He had two suitcases with him in the car. He was to park around a curve on San Yisidro, and wait to see whether he was followed."

"And what was intended to be done with the money?"

"He would leave it in the trunk of his car until we turned it over to be laundered."

"And who was going to launder it?"

Ranier hesitated now. Masuto waited. Then Ranier shrugged and said, "Hennesy."

"Ah, so!" It slipped out. He disliked the expression. "Then Hennesy was in on the kidnapping?"

"No. I mean, not to my knowledge. Mike hated him. The Angel could have told him, but I don't know. We were going to wait a few days until things quieted down, and then we'd make our deal with Hennesy."

"And how do you know Hennesy wouldn't blow the whole thing?"

"Hennesy? Come on, Sergeant. Mr. Hennesy has a reputation to uphold."

"What did Angel do when her husband didn't appear?"

"She waited for an hour, and then she took a cab. She dropped it a few blocks away and walked here to the house."

"You met her when she returned?"

"That's right. I opened the door for her, and as soon as I saw her without Mike, I knew that we'd screwed up. My first thought was that Mike had taken off with the money, but that made no sense. I told Angel to go up to her room and go into shock or something, and I'd call Dr. Haddam, and she wasn't to talk to anyone until we found out what had happened to Mike and the money."

"Where were McCarthy and Miss Newman when you spoke to Mrs. Barton?"

"He was in the living room. She was in the library. They came out while I was talking to Angel, and she threw a hysterical fit and rushed up to her room."

"You spoke to Mrs. Barton in the hallway at the door?"

"Yes."

"I presume they did not overhear you?"

"No. We were whispering."

"And why are you telling me all this, Mr. Ranier?"

"I told you before. I'm not going to take a murder rap. I know I'm the prime suspect. Sooner or later you'd find the key to my apartment in Angel's purse or somewhere. I said my secretary was in my office and saw me when I went back there. I lied. She wasn't there, so I have no alibi for the time I was away. And then that bitch Newman accused me of murdering Mike. You put it all together, and you got enough to bring it to the D.A. That's why I'm leveling with you."

Masuto regarded him thoughtfully for a few moments, and then he said, "I don't think you killed Mike Barton, Mr. Ranier, and I don't think you killed his wife."

"Well, thank God for that."

"I might still bring it to the D.A."

"Why? You just said you didn't think I killed either of them! You going to frame me?"

"Not for murder. There are other matters."

"What other matters? I've been stupid, but I committed no crime. There was no kidnapping as such. You can't indict me for a dumb trick."

"How about the million dollars?"

"I'll pay it back if I have to ruin myself. I'll be ruined anyway when this gets out."

"And conspiracy to defraud the government?"

"Come on, Masuto, you know you could never prove such a conspiracy. If you testified, I'd deny it. I made no confession."

"Well, that would depend on what the FBI decides. It's a federal matter. On the other hand, they might be willing to make a deal with you."

"What kind of a deal?"

"If you were willing to testify against Congressman Hennesy."

"My life wouldn't be worth a cent if I did. You know that."

"Well, it's up to you."

"Why don't you get Hennesy on this? He's always been crazy about Angel. She could have tipped him off, and then with Mike dead, they split a million between them."

"So you think Hennesy killed Barton?"

"Why not? It's a good guess."

"I think you should go home, Mr. Ranier. It's almost eleven o'clock."

8
Mrs. Holtz

They had all departed, the living and the dead, leaving Masuto alone in the house with the servants. He was tired and he was depressed. In its outer countenance, Beverly Hills was the most beautiful of cities—lovely palm-lined streets, immaculate lawns, splendid examples of every tropical plant that money could provide; and behind the façades of the million-dollar houses, a bitter commentary on the happiness that money buys. He thought about it for a while, and then he thought, as so often before, about giving it all up—and then wondered, as so often before, what else he could do. He had a profession, and he was very good at it, but it was too much like the pathology of Dr. Baxter; he cut and dissected and put the bits and pieces under his own peculiar microscope, and then he had to live with what he discovered.

He called his wife. She never asked when he would come home. The tone of his voice told her things. "You are unhappy and depressed," she said to him. "Has it been bad?"

His thought was that he struggled to retain some faith in the human race, and when that slipped away, it was very bad indeed. But he said, "Not too bad, Kati."

"I'll wait for you. You haven't eaten."

"How do you know that?"

"I know you."

He put down the telephone. A sliver of light gleamed from under the kitchen door, and Masuto went through the pantry and into the kitchen. Lena Jones sat at the kitchen table with Mrs. Holtz. Their teacups were empty. They just sat there.

"I wait until you leave," Mrs. Holtz said to Masuto, "then I lock up. Go to bed," she said to the black girl.

"I'm afraid."

"Nothing will harm you, so go to bed."

"I won't be able to sleep. I'm too scared."

"It's all right," Masuto told her gently. "No one will harm you now. Tell me, Lena, where were you when Mrs. Barton returned this afternoon?"

"Upstairs, cleaning Mr. Barton's room."

"Did you happen to look out of the window? The room is at the front of the house, isn't it?"

"I did look, yes."

"Why? Was there some special reason?"

"The window was open. I heard Mr. Kelly call out."

"From where? I mean, where was Kelly?"

"I guess in his room over the garage."

"And you heard his voice. What did he say?"

"I think, 'Hey, Angel.'"

"Angel? Not Mrs. Barton?"

"Once I heard him call her Angel," Mrs. Holtz said. "Like he was making fun of her."

"And from the window, you saw Mrs. Barton?"

Lena nodded. "Coming up the driveway. Walking slow, like she didn't hear Mr. Kelly at all."

"She didn't respond to his shout?"

"No."

"How did she look?"

"Terrible. She was dragging herself."

"Did you see a taxi pulling out of the driveway?"

Lena shook her head and began to sob.

"You go to bed," Mrs. Holtz said. "Right now, you go to bed."

Still sobbing, Lena Jones stood up and walked out of the kitchen.

"Sit down," Mrs. Holtz said to Masuto. "I make you a nice cup of tea. Or maybe coffee?"

"Tea will be fine."

She put a kettle of water on the stove and started the light under it. "A few minutes," she said. "Tell me, you like your tea strong like the British drink it or weak like the Americans drink it?"

"Weak."

"I'm sorry I don't have Japanese tea. It's green, yes?"

"Sometimes."

"And you're Japanese? I mean I know you was born here, the way you talk, and on the police."

"Yes, I'm Japanese. When we're born in America of Japanese parents, we're called nisei."

"I'm asking too many questions? I'm nosy?"

"Please feel free to ask me anything."

"Myself, I'm Polish. I was in a concentration camp." She pulled up her sleeve to show the tattoo mark. "I was a young girl. I don't like to talk about how I survived." As she spoke, she cut several slices of sponge cake and set the plate in front of Masuto. "Mike's favorite cake. Poor boy."

"It looks delicious," Masuto acknowledged. "But I'd rather not."

"Japanese don't eat cake?"

"Of course they do. But my wife is waiting up for me with dinner, and if I don't finish every bit of it, she'll be hurt."

"You're married! So if your wife is waiting, why don't you go home already?"

"Because I wanted to talk to you again, Mrs. Holtz."

"You give me credit for more brains than I have. Tell me something, I know you're not Jewish, so what are you, a Christian?"

"I'm a Buddhist."

She shook her head. "I think I heard about it, but I don't know what it is."

"It's a way of living, acting, being, of knowing who you are."

She poured the tea and placed it in front of him. "Sugar?" Masuto shook his head.

"So tell me, please, how do Buddhists feel about Jews?"

"The same way they would feel about any other people."

"And none of them hate Jews?"

"Buddhists try not to hate."

"That's nice." She sat at the table, facing him, a shapeless woman whose lined face was etched with suffering. "That's very nice, Mr. Masuto. Hate is so crazy, so unreasonable. Someone like Kelly, he has to hate Jews, he has to hate colored people, he has to make life miserable for poor Lena."

"I thought he was very fond of Mr. Barton."

Mrs. Holtz shrugged. "Not so fond. Sure, Mike was good to him. Maybe nobody was ever so good to Kelly as Mike. And Kelly liked his job. But he'd get mad at Lena and yell, 'Get that lousy Jew nigger out of here.' Then he'd complain about the Jew food I cooked. Not with Mike where Mike could hear him. And I'll tell you something else. He has a gun."

"How do you know?"

"Because Lena was cleaning his room and she saw it."

"Perhaps Mr. Barton wanted him to have a gun."

"Maybe. I don't know."

"We think," Masuto said, "that Mrs. Barton was blackmailing her husband. Miss Newman seems to feel that strongly. Do you have any notion of what she might have held over him?"

Mrs. Holtz shook her head. "They had terrible fights at first, and then, about a year ago, they stopped fighting."

"Do you know what the fights were about?"

"I wouldn't listen. I liked Mr. Barton too much. I couldn't bear to listen."

"Did Lena listen?"

"Lena's a good girl. She wouldn't listen."

"No, of course not," Masuto said, his tone easy and without threat. "But you yourself, Mrs. Holtz, you live here, you must have known what went on in this house."

"I'm not a spy," she said with annoyance.

"No, of course not. And I'm not talking about ordinary blackmail on Mrs. Barton's part. It was something she knew about him, or something about herself. Miss Newman indicated that it would wreck Mr. Barton's film career if it came out—and that this was the reason he stayed married to Angel."

"He must have had a reason. They weren't like a man and a wife. They had separate rooms. Sometimes for days they didn't even talk to each other."

"Was he in love with Elaine Newman?"

"You think Elaine killed Angel? You're crazy, Mr. Policeman."

"No, I don't think she killed Angel."

"She loved him, he loved her, that's a sin?"

"Did Angel know?"

"What do you think? She knew and she didn't care. She had Mike's money. She lived like a queen."

"Who do you think killed Mike Barton?"

Mrs. Holtz answered without hesitation. "Kelly. He killed both of them, and now Lena and me, we're here alone with him. Why don't you do something about that, Mr. Policeman?"

"I don't think you're in any danger, Mrs. Holtz. We'll have a policeman in the front hall all night, and tomorrow we'll go into the question of whether Kelly has a permit for the gun. Only one more question. Who were Angel Barton's friends?"

"Who could want to be her friend?"

"I'm sure she had friends. She was a beautiful woman. Who did she go out of her way to see?"

Mrs. Holtz thought about it for a while, her face set. Then she shrugged. "Maybe they were her friends."

"Who?"

"That congressman, Hennesy, and Netty Cooper."

Masuto had finished his tea. "Thank you," he said to her. "You've been helpful. Try to get a good night's sleep."

In the hallway, Officer Voorhis was dozing over a copy of *Sports Illustrated*. He blinked sleepily at Masuto. "I wasn't really asleep," he explained.

"Try being really awake."

It was a cold night for southern California, the temperature down to forty-five degrees. Masuto drove through a Beverly Hills as dark and empty as a city long forgotten and deserted, as dark and empty as a graveyard. Too much had happened in a single day; he couldn't cope with it or digest it properly, and he did what Zen had trained him to do. He emptied his mind of all thought and conjecture and let himself become one with his car, the dark streets and the night, along Olympic Boulevard and south on Motor Avenue to Culver City. It was a half hour past midnight when he pulled into the little driveway alongside his cottage, entered his house, and embraced Kati.

"It's so late. Why did you wait up for me?"

"Because my day doesn't finish until I see you. I have good things for tempura. It will only take a few minutes."

"I couldn't face real food now," Masuto said. "A boiled egg and some toast and tea."

"Then have your bath and it will be ready. The tub is full, and there are hot towels."

"The children are all right?"

"The children are fine. Ana won a prize for her ecology poster. She drew a beautiful picture of a deer. Do you think she will grow up to be an artist?"

Masuto laughed. It was good to be back in this world. "She is an artist," he said to Kati. "Perhaps we all begin as artists. Then it leaves us."

"Must it?"

"Perhaps not with Ana, if we are wise."

"It's very hard to be wise," Kati said.

"The hardest thing of all, yes."

"But much easier to be helpful. Have your bath and I'll prepare some food."

"In a moment. I want to step outside and look at the roses."

"In the dark?"

"There's a moon, and the smell is best at night. It's some small consolation, Kati. November is the best month for roses, and I've hardly looked at mine."

Of course they showed no color, even in the moonlight, but the air was full of the odor, subtly threading its way through the stronger scent of night-blooming jasmine. The rose garden was Masuto's hobby, his delight, his own proof that even as a policeman he retained some small trace of the artist. His backyard was small, thirty feet wide and forty feet deep, but he needed no more space than that. Except for the explosive climbers that made a fence around the yard, the roses were spare, skeletonlike stems that burst into a variety of glory. That appealed to Masuto—the thorny stems and the marvelous blooms of color and scent.

He stayed with the rosebushes a few minutes, but it was enough. Then he went into the house and had his bath.

9
The Zendo

When Masuto's universe was too greatly askew, when the face of reality dissolved into too many grotesques, he would rise early in the morning and drive to the Zendo for meditation. Ordinarily, he did his meditation each morning in his tiny room in the house; but to meditate with others in a place given to meditation was more gratifying. Now, dressed, he kissed Kati gently. She opened her eyes and complained that it was still dark.

"It's half past six. I go to the Zendo first."

"The children won't see you," she said plaintively.

"Perhaps I can get home early this evening. I promise to try."

The Zendo was in downtown Los Angeles, a cluster of half a dozen once-dilapidated California bungalows that the students and monks who lived there had restored. All around it was the decay and disintegration of the inner city. The dawn light was just beginning when Masuto parked his car in front of the Zendo, and then as he stepped out, he felt himself grabbed in a tight embrace from behind. A second young man appeared in front of him, put a knife to his stomach, and said,

"Just take it easy, turkey." Then, still holding the knife to Masuto's stomach, he pulled aside his jacket and saw Masuto's gun. "Son of a bitch, the chink's a cop! We got us a fuzz!"

Masuto felt the grip around his arms slacken for just an instant, enough for him to drive his elbow into the ribcage of the man behind him, at the same time, pivoting, so that the knife thrust intended for him took the man who was holding him in the side. The wounded man screamed and let go of him, and Masuto leaped away with his gun out.

Fifteen minutes later, a squad car drove away with one of the muggers, while an ambulance carried off the second one, and Masuto found himself abashedly and uncomfortably facing a group of monks in their brown robes. They made no comment, and Masuto, who was trying to frame an explanation or apology in his own mind, found none that would do. Whereupon, he bent his head and walked into the meditation hall. Half a dozen people were still there, sitting cross-legged on cushions on the two slightly raised platforms that ran the length of the room. At one end of the room, the old rashi, the Japanese Zen master, sat in meditation. The half dozen included two monks, a young, pretty woman, and three middle-aged men who looked like business executives. Masuto took off his shoes and joined them, his folded hands still shaking from his experience. He tried to fall into the meditation, but after what had happened outside, it was very difficult.

One by one, the other meditators finished, made their bow to the rashi, and left, until only Masuto and the old man remained. Masuto's half-closed eyes were fixed on the floor in front of him. He heard the rashi move, and then the old man's feet, encased in straw slippers, appeared in front of him. Masuto looked up.

"You bring violence with you," the rashi said, speaking Japanese.

"It met me on the street outside."

"Ask yourself where it came from."

"I am deeply sorry. I disturbed the peace of this place."

"Are you all right?"

"I am not hurt, if that's what you mean."

"I can see that you're not hurt."

"Then I must answer no."

"Then look into yourself. Even a policeman can know why he is a policeman."

"I will try, honorable rashi."

Leaving the Zendo, Masuto realized that he was ravenously hungry, and he pulled into a short order place on Olympic. Bacon and eggs and fried potatoes and four slices of bread and two cups of coffee helped to restore his equanimity. It was ten minutes to nine when he arrived at the station house. Beckman was waiting for him, along with Frank Keller, the FBI man.

"Your hunch was pretty good," Keller said to Masuto. "And this is confidential as hell, but we've been running an investigation on Hennesy for the past seven months. The Coast Guard grabbed a boat off San Diego and picked up a kilo of cocaine. Hennesy's name was in the boat's log. It could be another Roy Hennesy, because the name's not that uncommon, but when you put it together with the other tidbits about Hennesy's moral stance, it could mean something. The department's cooking up a move against a number of public officials who are a little less than kosher, and they don't want anything to upset the apple cart. So unless you tie him in directly to kidnap or murder, they'd just as soon let him be."

"Have you ever known the goddamn feds not to tell you to keep hands off?" Beckman said with annoyance.

"Forget it," Masuto said.

"I'll be at my office downtown," Keller said, his feelings bruised. He stalked out.

"You don't have to lean on him," Masuto told Beckman. "He's a decent kid, for a fed."

"What have you been drinking, the milk of human kindness? Anyway, the captain wants to see you right off. He's in his office with Dr. Haddam—the one who came to see the Angel."

"Out at Malibu," Masuto asked him, "what kind of a dress was Netty Cooper wearing?"

"What?"

"Come on, think."

"It was sort of like a kimono, pale green."

"Yes. Long sleeves? Enough to hide needle marks?"

"I think so."

"Good. Wait for me. This can't take too long."

In Wainwright's office Dr. Haddam was protesting. He was a neat, stout little man, with steel-rimmed glasses, bald, and a high-pitched voice that proclaimed his irritation. "I find this whole thing highly annoying, if not unethical. Why didn't you call me when Mrs. Barton died? I'm the family physician. The family—"

"I told you before, Doctor, there is no family. They are both dead. We have no indication of family beyond that. This is Detective Sergeant Masuto."

"Then I wash my hands of the whole matter."

"Yes, if you wish. But we'd like to ask you a few questions."

"I don't have to answer any questions. Indeed, I don't intend to. I'm a busy man. Call my nurse, make an appointment, and if I can find the time, I will talk to you."

He started to leave, and Wainwright said evenly, "A hypodermic syringe which contained something that was apparently the cause of Mrs. Barton's death was found beside her. Since you were the doctor in attendance, this puts you in an awkward position. Surely you realize that."

The doctor stopped short, turned slowly to face Wainwright, and growled—a valid growl for so short a man. "How dare you! That, sir, is actionable! I'm a practicing physician and a resident of Beverly Hills for twenty-five years, and you dare—"

"Please, sir," Masuto said, spreading his hands, "you read an implication that was not there. We found the hypodermic and Mrs. Barton is dead. We simply must ask you the circumstances of your visit to her."

"You found a hypodermic!" he snorted. "What was in it? What caused her death? Why didn't you call me then?"

"We don't know what caused her death," Wainwright said.

"The autopsy is being performed right now at All Saints Hospital."

"You don't know! And you call yourselves police!"

"What did you do for Mrs. Barton?" Masuto asked. "What condition was she in? What did you prescribe?"

"I prescribed nothing."

"Oh?"

"Nothing."

"Did you examine her?"

"No. She wouldn't let me near her. In fact, that ill-natured woman drove me out of the room."

"But you were her physician."

"I was Mr. Barton's physician. Now I shall tell you what happened, and that's the end of it. Mr. McCarthy asked me to see her. I went into her bedroom, and she snarled at me to get out—and used very abusive language, I may add. There are sides to that Angel the public never saw. Then Mr. McCarthy went into the room, and I heard her snapping at him. She threw a shoe at him as he left. She slammed the door after him. Then the maid appeared with a tall glass of ice and apparently Scotch whisky. I would presume at least four ounces of whisky over the ice. She said that their butler or chauffeur, what is his name?"

"Kelly."

"Kelly. Yes, he had sent it up. Then Angel opened the door, took the glass, and so help me God, drained down most of it."

"You were standing in the hall?" Masuto asked.

"Yes, with McCarthy. The maid was at the door. Mrs. Barton handed her the glass and slammed the door in our faces. Then I left. She did not strike me as a woman who required either a sedative or an examination. A psychiatrist, perhaps. Now you have my story, and I would like to leave."

"Of course," Masuto said. "You've been very helpful. We are most grateful."

"Well, there you are," Wainwright said, after the doctor had departed. "Unless he's lying."

"No, he's telling the truth. He knows we can check it out

with McCarthy. He's a doctor, not an actor, and that beautiful indignation could not be manufactured."

"Do you suppose Kelly killed her?"

"I don't know."

"You don't know. When this thing was ten minutes old, you told me you knew who killed Barton. Has your Chinese crystal ball collapsed?"

"Even Sweeney no longer classes all Orientals as Chinese—"

"Get off your high horse, Masao. They're all leaning on me, like we were Scotland Yard instead of a two-bit small-town police force."

"It was only yesterday. We're making progress."

"Tell me about it."

"What the good doctor told us helps."

"That's bullshit, Masao, and you know it, and I know how you work. You got something, and you're not opening your mouth about it. Now, I'll tell you what I'm going to do. I'm going to search that Barton house from cellar to attic, and I'm going to find that million dollars."

"It's not there."

"How the hell do you know?"

"Because I think I know where it is. Now, wait a moment," he said as Wainwright began to explode. "Just hold on. That doesn't mean I know where it is."

"Then what in hell does it mean?"

"It means that I could make a guess, and then if we act on my guess and go ahead and get a search warrant and search the place and find nothing, we'd be in for a lawsuit that would make your year's budget look like peanuts."

"All right, tell me—no, the hell with you. Get out of here and make this thing make sense."

"When will Baxter finish the autopsy?"

"He says by noon." Masuto started for the door. "One thing," Wainwright added, "how does Kelly figure?"

"I don't know."

"He's a part of it?"

"I think so."

As if he had heard the question, Beckman entered the office as Wainwright was saying, "Maybe I'm a cynical old cop, but I never trusted a reformed ex-con."

"You mean Kelly?" Beckman asked.

"That's right. I mean Kelly."

"Well, Dempsy just called. He took over at the Barton place from Voorhis, and he says that the ladies are worried because Kelly didn't show this morning and Kelly's place over the garage is locked, and what should he do?"

"Tell him to do nothing," Wainwright said. "You two get over there, and let me know what you find. If Kelly skipped with that million, you will have a hell of a lot of explaining to do."

"What did he mean by that?" Beckman asked Masuto as they left the building.

"He wants to search the Barton place. If Kelly skipped with the money, he'll blame us for not searching the place yesterday."

"Do you think he did?"

"No."

"Then where is he?"

"I imagine he's right there in his room."

"Come on, you know Dempsy. He'd pound on the door and yell loud enough to wake the dead."

"Nobody yells loud enough to wake the dead. Take your car, Sy. I'll follow you to the house."

"Wait a minute, Masao—what are you trying to tell me? That Kelly is dead?"

"Perhaps. Civilization, or what we have of it, stops short at a million dollars. It's a strong inducement."

10

The Loser

Officer Dempsy was waiting in the driveway when Masuto and Beckman pulled their cars up in front of the garage. A TV unit was there, photographing the house, and one of the men in the unit recognized Masuto and came over to ask whether there were any new developments.

"Not that I know of," Masuto said. "Anyway, I don't do the P.R. You know that. They'll give you the story over at headquarters."

"You know they give me nothing. Anyway, we want pictures. If I could talk to the servants?"

"Absolutely not."

"I don't have to talk to them. Let us photograph them."

"No."

He went back to his unit, and Dempsy said, "They've been driving me crazy, Sergeant. Anyway, the two ladies are too scared to come out of the house, and I wouldn't let them in."

"Good. Now where's Voorhis?"

"Home, sleeping."

"Wake him up and get him over here. Now, as I understand it, Kelly's place is over the garage."

"That's right."

"Two entrances," Beckman said. "I checked it out yesterday. There's one door at the top of that staircase outside"—he pointed to the farther wall of the garage—"and another at the end of a passageway on the top floor of the house. Same passageway leads to Mrs. Holtz's room and the maid's room. Both doors have those locks with the little thing in the handle. You turn it, and then you can close the door from the outside and it's locked. No keys. I asked Kelly about that. He said there never were any keys while he worked here."

"You tried both doors?" Masuto asked Dempsy.

"Sure. The doors are the kind you can kick in, but I didn't want to try that until you gave the word."

"What do you think, Masao?" Beckman asked. "Can we force entrance, or will we be asking for trouble?"

"Who from? Both owners are dead, and if Kelly's alive, why would he lock the doors?"

"Do you have sufficient cause?"

"A man could be half dead in there. That's sufficient cause."

Before they went into the house, Masuto said to Dempsy, "No media inside the house. If Ranier or McCarthy or any other friends of the Bartons show up, tell them to wait and get me. And when Voorhis arrives, I want to see him. Now get him over here."

Masuto and Beckman went into the house and through to the kitchen. The two women turned from their work to stare woefully at the detectives.

"What happens now, Mr. Masuto?" Mrs. Holtz wanted to know.

"We'll see. I want to get into Kelly's room. I'm told there are no keys."

"That's right. Kelly never asked for them. He said he didn't need them, so Mr. Barton never had them made."

"Is it a single room?"

"No, two rooms, a bedroom and a little sitting room. The outside door is into the sitting room. Kelly always kept that locked, but he never locked the door into the hall upstairs."

"But we hardly ever went into his rooms," Lena said. "When we had to go in there and clean, it made him mad. He tell us to stay out, with a lot of badmouth talk."

"Mrs. Holtz," Masuto said, "I have to address you as the caretaker of the house, simply because there's no one else responsible. I'm informing you that I have good reason to believe that Kelly is injured and requires help. I want you to understand that considering these circumstances, I shall break down the door."

Mrs. Holtz sighed and shrugged. "If you must, you must."

"Servants' quarters," Beckman said as he led Masuto up the kitchen stairs and into a shabby hallway. "Four rooms here, and Kelly's place. I guess they don't build them like this anymore. That's it," he said, pointing to the door at the end of the hall."

"Kick it in, Sy."

Beckman raised his size fourteen shoe and let go at the door. It flew open, the bolt tearing out of the jamb, and they walked into Kelly's bedroom. There was a single bed, neatly made up, and pasted on the wall, several tear sheets from skin magazines.

"Super neat, some of these ex-cons," Beckman said.

Masuto opened the door to the sitting room. Kelly sat in an ancient armchair, a crooked smile on his face, his eyes wide open. There was a bullet hole in the center of his forehead.

"Poor bastard," Beckman said. "Poor dumb loser."

"It was his karma."

"Spends the best years of his life in jail and ends up like this, hates the whole world, hates Jews, hates blacks, and the poor dumb bastard never knew what he was doing."

"That's it. He never knew what he was doing."

"Why?" Beckman wondered. "Why did they kill him?"

"He wanted some of the million dollars. Probably, he didn't want too much. He was always a petty thief. But whatever he wanted, it was more than his life was worth."

"The same killer?"

"No, I don't think so," Masuto said slowly. "We have three murders, and we have three murderers."

"Come on, Masao, why? Why three?"

"Because I think I know who two of them are, and neither of them could have killed Kelly."

"I'll call the captain. What about Doc Baxter? He's doing the Angel's autopsy."

"I want him here. I want to know when Kelly died. Tell the captain that, and let him fight it out with Baxter."

For a while after Beckman had left, Masuto stood staring at the dead man. It would be comfortable, he felt, to believe, as his ancestors had, that people lived many lives, and that perhaps in one of them Kelly would have found some peace. Now three people were dead, a simple, bloody case of greed—vulgar and grotesque.

Masuto went back into the bedroom and opened the top drawer of the old chest that served as Kelly's wardrobe. He pushed aside underwear and a rumpled shirt, and there was Kelly's gun, an ancient automatic pistol, rusted and clogged in the barrel. When he had worked out the clip, he saw that it was empty. If anyone had tried to fire the gun, it would have blown up in his face, a gun that Kelly had picked up somewhere, perhaps in a garbage dump. Aside from the gun, the two small rooms revealed nothing that could relate in any way to his death. No writing, no pens, no pencils. Perhaps Kelly had been illiterate. There were half a dozen magazines, *Playboy, Penthouse,* two suits in the closet, a pair of sneakers, an extra pair of shoes, a razor and shaving cream on the sink in the tiny bathroom and only aspirin and a laxative in the medicine chest. A plant with several red geranium blossoms served as the only touch of color or decoration.

Masuto closed his eyes and stood silently until he heard steps in the passageway. It was Beckman returning, and with him, Officer Voorhis.

"Oh, Jesus," Voorhis said. "When did that happen?"

"While you were on duty last night. What happened, Voorhis, did you fall asleep?"

"Sergeant, I swear to God—"

"I don't want that!" Masuto snapped at him. "I want to know whether you fell asleep, and I want the truth!"

"Jesus, Sarge, this place was quiet as a tomb. Maybe I dozed a little, but I didn't sleep."

"You can explain the difference another time. Where were you?"

"In the front hall."

"Did you go out and patrol the grounds?"

"Yes."

"How many times?"

Voorhis hesitated.

"The truth," Masuto said.

"Once."

"Great. Just great. And when was that?"

"About an hour after you left."

"So from one o'clock until Dempsy relieved you, you just sat in the hall and dozed, as you put it. You didn't sleep, you dozed. That's a damn easy way to earn your pay."

"I told you it was quiet as a tomb. Nothing moved."

"When you were awake or when you were sleeping? Never mind. Did you hear anything, the shot, the sound of a car?"

"Nothing, Sarge. I never heard a sound."

"Beautiful!" Beckman exploded. "You're one smart cop, Voorhis. You're put on duty to guard a house and a murder takes place right under your nose."

"For Christ's sake, what am I, a platoon? I was in the front hall. There's an outside entrance to this place, and whoever killed him must have used a silencer. The ladies didn't hear anything, so why are you leaning on me?"

"All right, Voorhis," Masuto said. "Go back to the station and write out your report." And to Beckman, "The ladies heard nothing?"

"Nothing. And the walls and doors in this servants' wing are paper thin. So he must have used a silencer."

"I suppose so."

"That's a steady hand. A gun with a silencer and pop—right

between the eyes. That's very professional shooting, Masao, and cool too. It wouldn't be a contract, would it?"

"Not likely. There just hasn't been time enough to set something up. This is the result of what happened yesterday." Masuto peered closely at Kelly. "No powder burns. He probably stood across the room. Sy," he said, turning to Beckman, "I want you to go out to Malibu and search the Barton place. You'll have to sweet-talk Cominsky to get in there, but I don't think he'll mind."

"He searched it, you know."

"But he wasn't looking for something."

"What am I looking for? The million dollars?"

"No, it's not there."

"Then what?"

"I don't know," Masuto said.

"But not like Cominsky, I'm looking for something. Only I don't know what."

"That's right."

"If you say so."

"And one more thing. After that, Sy, I want the war records, if any, of McCarthy, Goldberg, Ranier, and Hennesy. I want to know what they were in the service—rank, division, job, whatever you can come up with."

"And who took commendations for pistol marksmanship?"

"That would help."

"And where will you be?"

"Here, I suppose. Or at the station."

Only a few moments after Beckman left, Captain Wainwright stalked in, followed by Sweeney with his fingerprint kit, Amos Silver, the police photographer, and Dr. Baxter, who said cheerfully, "Live in Beverly Hills. A short life but a merry one. What goodie do you have for me now?"

Masuto pointed to Kelly's corpse, visible through the door to the next room.

"Went out with a smile," Baxter said. "Few of them do."

"You're a damned ghoul," Wainwright muttered.

"Pathology, dear Captain, is a ghoulish business. Let's have a look at him. Would it surprise you if I said he died of severe trauma of the brain? No, it would not. No powder marks. I'd say the shot was fired from at least ten feet. Took the back off the skull, perhaps a thirty-eight. And of course you whiz kids are waiting for me to tell you when he died. Not easy. Not easy at all," Baxter complained, flexing Kelly's fingers and feeling his cheeks. "At least six hours. That's the best I can do."

"Which would put it back to four o'clock in the morning."

"Give or take an hour."

"And when you autopsy," Masuto asked, "you can certainly pin it down more closely?"

"Ah, the autopsy. Just happen to be in the midst of an utterly fascinating autopsy—one Angel Barton."

"What have you got?" Wainwright demanded. "What killed her?"

"Ah, there's a question," Baxter said, smiling impishly. "But, you see, I am not quite through, and not one word until I finish. I'll have some surprises, depend on it. Tell you what, send our Oriental wizard over to the hospital in an hour or so, and I'll give him chapter and verse. Now I'm on my way— unless there are any other questions about the deceased?"

When Baxter had departed, Wainwright asked, "Why do I hate that man?"

"He's a good pathologist," Masuto said. "I suppose it's just his nature to be nasty."

"Have you searched the place?"

"Nothing that means anything. As Beckman said, the poor devil's a loser—all his life. This gun was in a drawer of the chest."

"This gun can't be fired. Why do you suppose he hung on to an old piece of junk?"

"It probably gave him a sense of security."

The photographer finished his work, telling them, "I'll have prints in an hour or two." The ambulance men arrived as the photographer left, straightened Kelly's body with difficulty, and carried him out.

"I hate this," Wainwright muttered. "I hate this whole case. Is there any hope of winding it up, Masao?"

"Tonight perhaps."

"You got to be kidding."

"No. I know who killed Barton—"

"His wife? How the hell do you ever prove that? She's dead."

"You're right. I don't think we'll ever prove it, and if she weren't dead, I don't think we could ever convict her. I'm not sure we could convict the other two—"

"Two of them?"

"I think so. One killed Angel, and someone else killed Kelly. We have three murders, three murderers."

"Beautiful—that's just beautiful." He stared at Masuto. "I never know when you're telling me something you know or handing me a line of crap. You think you can clean this up tonight?"

"I think so, yes."

"All right, who killed Angel and who killed Kelly?"

"I think I know who killed Angel. Kelly . . ." He shook his head. "But if you can get them here tonight, I think I can give it to you. Kelly and Angel both."

"Who? Get who here? How do you get people here? Are you indulging in some goddamn literary detective fantasy?"

"McCarthy, Ranier, the Goldbergs, Mrs. Cooper, Miss Newman, and Hennesy."

"Masao, have you lost your bearings. You don't do such things."

"It can be done."

"How? Do I arrest them? Do I kidnap them?"

"Have someone reach each one of them and tell them that tonight we are going to expose the killers. You can't force them to come, but they'll come."

"You read that in a book."

"I don't read murder mysteries," Masuto said with some annoyance. "It's bad enough that I live with it. Do you want me to read about it as well?"

"I read them," Sweeney said. "You put them in one room and you get the killer. It's pure bullshit. Every time I read one of them, I ask myself why those clowns don't take a look at the way ordinary cops work. Like crawling around this place looking for fingerprints. From what I see, this Kelly never had a visitor. All the prints match up."

"With what?" Wainwright demanded. "How the hell do you know that they match up?"

"Because," Sweeney replied, smiling thinly, "when you tell me this joker has a record, which was yesterday, I pull a set of prints from the Los Angeles cops and I got it right here with me."

"Yeah, you're a real smartass cop," Wainwright said and, turning to Masuto, "I don't like it. Anyway, how can you be sure they'll come?"

"I'm not sure. But look at it this way, Captain. There are two draws—curiosity and guilt. These people like to talk, and this is something to talk about, something to make them shine at a dinner party or whatever. On the other hand, the guilty ones will feel they're pointing to themselves if they don't show."

"And how about this Angel business, Masao? Do you really think you know who killed her?"

"I'm guessing. I could be wrong."

"And when you get them here, what then?"

"I think I know a way."

"You're sure it's one of them?"

"Two of them," Masuto said. "Will you give it a try?"

"All right. But I'll be going way out on a limb, and so help me God, Masao, if you leave me hanging there, I'll take it out of your hide. What time?"

"Let's say nine o'clock. And I'll need some money."

"What do you mean, you'll need some money?"

"You'll get it back."

"When?"

"Tonight."

"All of it?" Wainwright asked suspiciously. "What the hell is it for if I get all of it back?"

"Trust me, please."

"How much?"

"A thousand dollars."

Wainwright regarded Masuto sourly. "All right. But I want it back, every cent of it. I'm going to the station house now, and I'll pull a draft for you and you can cash it at the bank. Are you going to call these characters?"

"If you could do it," Masuto said gently, "it would be much more meaningful. You've got the rank and they'll be impressed with a call from you."

Wainwright stared at him, shook his head, turned on his heel, and walked out. Sweeney, putting his equipment together, looked at Masuto with respect. "That was beautiful," he said. "That was like Moses getting water from a rock. The captain will never be the same again."

"I think he took it very well."

"Look, Sarge, do you expect any significant prints from this place?"

"No."

"Then why the hell do you let me work my ass off?"

"You're fingerprints. If you don't look for fingerprints, the captain would be very upset. You know that."

"The hell with you!" Sweeney said, and stalked out. A minute or so later, Masuto followed him.

Downstairs in the kitchen Mrs. Holtz and Lena Jones sat at the kitchen table, depleted, their faces full of hopeless fear. Elaine Newman stood at a window, staring at the gardens behind the house. She had come there while Masuto was upstairs in Kelly's quarters, and now as he entered the kitchen, she turned slowly to face him.

"Will it stop? Will you ever stop it?"

"It's over now."

"I didn't know a thing like this could happen here—in America—in Beverly Hills. How can such a thing happen here?" Mrs. Holtz said.

"I just don't know what to do," Elaine said to Masuto. "What do you do? Do we keep the house going? Do we close it up? Who pays the wages of Mrs. Holtz and Lena—yes, and myself. I know it's selfish and unfeeling to talk about such things, but what am I supposed to do?"

"Did you call McCarthy? Wasn't he Barton's lawyer?"

"I called him. He doesn't return my calls. He isn't very fond of me."

Masuto went to her and put his arm around her shoulders. "We'll finish it soon," he said softly. "You've been through your own hell, but that will end." Suddenly, her face was pressed into his jacket and she was sobbing uncontrollably. He held her like that for a moment or two, and then he said, Will you help me? I need your help."

"Yes."

He took out his handkerchief and handed it to her, and she dried her eyes.

"Where do you work, Elaine? I mean in what room?" He quite deliberately called her by her first name. Masuto was not unaware of the fact that he was a very good-looking man, that women liked him and trusted him.

"Suppose we go there now. We'll talk." He turned to Mrs. Holtz and Lena Jones. "Don't be afraid. We have a policeman in the front hall. Let him answer the door."

"Will you be here?" Lena Jones asked desperately.

"For a little while. But the policeman will be here all day."

"You can't blame them," Elaine said as they walked to the library. "They're frightened. So am I. They live here. Where can they go?"

Dempsy was in the front hall. "Listen," Masuto said to him. "There are two women in the house, in the kitchen. I want you to look in there every half hour or so, make them feel comfortable. They're afraid."

"Sure."

"And no one else comes into the house—no one. Except Miss Newman here. If she leaves, she can return. But no one else. And if anyone gets nasty about it, call the captain."

She led Masuto into the library. It was more or less a standard Beverly Hills library or den, with wood-paneled walls, shelves of leather-bound books, tufted leather furniture, and bad pictures. There was a large desk and a typewriter.

"Sit down, please," Masuto said to her.

She curled up in one corner of the couch. Masuto sat facing her. "I'm all right now," she said.

"I know. You're a survivor."

"A woman alone in this town who isn't a survivor—well, I don't have to tell you."

"No, you don't. Now, you were here when Mike Barton left with the ransom money?"

"Yes. I told you that."

"How big was the suitcase?"

"Oh, about this size." She motioned with her hands. "You know the size you can bring on the plane with you? Well, I'd say it was a size larger."

"Is it one of a matched set?"

"Yes, it is."

"Could I see the set? Where would it be?"

"In the closet in Mike's room. I'll take you there." She led the way upstairs. Unlike Angel's room, this was plain, almost drab. The closet was a large, walk-in affair with, Masuto reflected, enough suits, jackets, and slacks to outfit the entire Beverly Hills police force. The luggage was lined up on a shelf, a space showing where one of the suitcases had been removed. Masuto pulled out the one next to it and studied it. "Just one of each size?"

"Yes, in that design, just one of each size. There are other suitcases in the storeroom."

"The same design?"

"Oh, no, quite different."

"Do you know where they came from?"

"They're from Gucci."

"The place on Rodeo Drive?"

"Exactly."

"Do you suppose they'd have another just like it?"

"I'm sure they would. It's a standard item."

"Well, that helps. Would you mind coming with me to Gucci to make sure I get the right thing?"

"Sure, if it's going to end this business."

"I think it will."

At Gucci's, fifteen minutes later, Elaine selected the suitcase.

"How much is it?" Masuto asked.

The clerk, who had been observing Masuto's creaseless gray flannels, his old tweed jacket, and his tieless shirt, said coldly, "Four hundred and twenty dollars."

Masuto responded with stunned silence, and Elaine stepped into the gap and said, "This is Sergeant Masuto of the Beverly Hills police force. We need the suitcase only for a single day, not for travel purposes, but simply as an exhibit."

Masuto took out his badge. "It will be returned, undamaged, tomorrow."

"I'll have to speak to the manager," the clerk said, and when the manager was apprised of the situation, he told them that he was delighted to be of some service to the Beverly Hills police. "You might mention the name Gucci," he said, "but only if it's convenient."

Outside, Masuto said to Elaine, "You, my dear, are a remarkable young woman."

"I think you're a remarkable cop," she returned.

11

The Autopsy

Masuto deposited the Gucci suitcase in the trunk of his car and drove Elaine back to the Barton house, explaining on the way about the proceedings scheduled for that evening. "I want things to be as loose and easy as possible. Mrs. Holtz can have cake and coffee for those who want it. Can Miss Jones mix drinks?"

"I'll help her. But what makes you so sure they'll come?"

"They'll come. This is not simply Beverly Hills, it's the American dream factory. Each one of them has either a starring or a supporting role, and they wouldn't miss it."

"And that's what the suitcase is for?"

"Perhaps. You know, Miss Newman, there is a Zen belief that what one sees is illusion. The reality is what one refuses to see."

"Yes, and now it's Miss Newman again."

"I'm a policeman."

"And married?"

"And married."

"They always are."

Leaving her at the house, Masuto drove to All Saints Hospital and made his way down a flight of steps to the basement and the pathology rooms. Dr. Baxter was waiting to welcome him with a malicious smile.

"Finished, Doctor?" Masuto asked pleasantly.

"I, my Oriental wizard, am finished. You have just begun."

"I am sure you will make it less difficult for me."

"Oh, no. No, indeed. I intend to make it damned confusing for you. Not with Mike Barton. A simple case of a bullet in the head, twenty-two caliber. Not with Mr. Kelly, whose skull was blown open with a thirty-eight. But with the Angel—ah, there we have a nest of worms."

"You know what killed her?"

"You're damn right I do. I'm a pathologist, not a cop. Would you like to hear what killed her?"

"Very much."

"Good. Then come over here and have a look at the body of the deceased. Having seen only one puncture hole on the arm of the deceased, you Sherlocks concluded that the Angel was not a user. Nothing of the kind. In her circle it is not fashionable to mark the arm. She used her thighs."

Masuto turned away, and Baxter covered the body. "Squeamish, huh? Now let me tell you what killed her. It was a combination of three things—Scotch whisky, chloral hydrate, and a large dose of heroin."

"Chloral hydrate?"

"The venerable Mickey Finn. My guess is that it was mixed into the whisky, which would put her to sleep, and while she was in slumberland, someone not concerned about marking the beautiful arm slipped in and shot her full of heroin."

Masuto made no response to this, his carefully constructed puzzle tilting and crumbling, and Baxter watched him with satisfaction. Then his usually impassive face creased in unhappiness, and he whispered, "Oh, my God, what a fool I was."

"Not alone, young fellow," Baxter said cheerfully, "not alone by any means. One among many, because now comes the whammy. Brace yourself." Silent, Masuto stared at him. "You can't guess? Come on, throw a wild one at me."

"I don't know what the devil you're talking about," Masuto said tiredly.

"Kind of upset you with that three-way knockout. By the way, any one of those three, the Mickey, the whisky, or the heroin would probably not be lethal. Put them together, and you have a one-way ticket into the great beyond. Still waiting for the whammy?"

"Yes, my good doctor," Masuto said coldly.

"Okay, here it is. Your Angel is not a woman. She's a man." Pleased with himself, he waited for Masuto's reaction.

"Is this another manifestation of what passes for your sense of humor?"

"Really getting to you today," Baxter said, rubbing his hands together. "As a matter of fact, it's pretty damn funny, isn't it?"

"You are the coldest, most inhuman imitation of a healer I have ever encountered!" Masuto said angrily.

"Healer? Hell, no. I am a pathologist, sonny, and don't you ever forget that—and a damn good one. And what I said before goes. Your Angel is a man."

"All right, I'm listening." His anger passed. Now the last few pieces were falling into place. "Please explain it."

"Have you ever heard of sexual reassignment?"

"You mean the medical change of a man into a woman?"

"Exactly. There have been half a dozen notorious cases and several thousand that the public never hears about. Now you take our Angel here. A rather small, delicately built man, not a homosexual, decides that he's a woman in a man's body. Some authorities feel it's a fixation. Others that it's a genetic error at birth. He goes to Denmark or France—or even up here to Stanford—where they've been doing it lately."

"Just what do they do?" Masuto asked.

"You want the whole thing?"

"Yes."

"All right. It begins with chemotherapy procedure. There are two families of hormones that play a major role in determining who is a man and who is a woman, the androgens and the estrogens. Both are present in both sexes, but in a man the androgens predominate and in a woman the estrogens predominate. The first step in sexual reassignment is to reverse the role and put the man on massive doses of estrogens. That starts a biochemical process of change. The male functions cease. The growth of the beard slows, the hips become rounded, then the entire musculature takes on a feminine aspect. Even the breasts begin to increase."

"Just from the hormones?"

"You're damn right, just from the hormones. But that's just the beginning. Electrolysis takes care of the beard. That's permanent. Then we go into the operating room. Silicone discs are implanted in the breasts. And then they do something called a bilateral orchiectomy, which, without going into details mean the changing of a man into a woman through operative procedure, removal of the testes and the conversion of the penis into an artificial vagina—and that's what you have lying there on my table, a woman who was once a man. Would you like to have another look?"

Masuto nodded, and once again Baxter removed the rubber sheet that covered Angel Barton's body. Even after having listened to Baxter's detailed lecture, Masuto found it hard to believe that he was not looking at the body of a beautiful woman. Watching him, Baxter said, "You start with a very handsome young man, you get a beautiful woman."

"Could she have intercourse?"

"After a fashion."

"What does that mean?"

"She's altered. That doesn't make her a whole woman. We're not God."

"Then eventually Mike Barton would have known."

"Unless he was a total idiot."

"Poor fool in a kingdom of fools," Masuto muttered. "The idol of millions married to a man who became a woman—his terrible secret. What clowns we are. That was his word. The only word. The proper word. How could he let the world know?"

Baxter covered the body. "Not a bad day's work. As for our movie star, he danced—and he paid the piper."

"I would appreciate it if you could sit on this for twenty-four hours."

"I'll be delighted to cooperate," Baxter said. His victory had almost mellowed him, but he could not resist adding, "I regret that I haven't handed you the killers on the same silver platter, but the city does pay you gentlemen for service."

Masuto departed without replying. His car was parked behind the hospital in the lot, but he felt a need to walk, and as he walked, circling away from the hospital and toward Sunset Boulevard, he once again contemplated the ridiculous anomaly of a Zen Buddhist policeman in Beverly Hills. Why did he go on with it? Why did he continue? What kind of karma brought him to this ultimate barbarism which was also the glittering crown of a monied civilization. These were questions he had proposed a hundred times before. They always remained unanswered.

He walked back to his car and drove to his home in Culver City. It was only one o'clock, and Kati was both alarmed and delighted.

"This is my spiritual and physical nourishment for today. I have eaten wretched food, and tonight I shall not be home before midnight. I have a half hour, dear Kati. Can you prepare something?"

It was a sudden descent and an imposition. She had just fed her two children and sent them back to school, and now she was in the midst of her ironing. The nisei women in her consciousness-raising class, which she had begun to attend a full year ago, would have voted to send Masuto out to a lunch stand. But since none of them were witness, Kati embraced her husband, and after she had assured herself that no injury or other tragedy had sent him home, prepared the tempura from the night before with amazing speed.

She sat opposite him, watching him eat. In spite of her consciousness-raising class, it was her pleasure to watch him eat.

"We live in a wilderness," he said.

"It's those terrible murders. I was listening to the news this morning, after the children left for school."

"Death is always terrible. But this is a sickness."

"Why do they do it, Masao?"

"Money, hatred, revenge."

"It frightens me so," Kati said. "Not because I expect anything to happen to me. I'm not afraid of such things. I wasn't afraid of that skinny Chicano boy who was such a foolish burglar. But because I lose my faith in the whole world."

"One should neither have faith nor lose faith. What is faith? This is the way things are."

"But why? Why are things this way?"

"Because we lose touch with what is real and then we invent what is not real."

"That's Zen talk," Kati said with irritation. "I don't understand it."

"Perhaps I don't understand it myself," Masuto said gently. "I need a few minutes to myself, a few minutes to sit and meditate."

But Kati's food helped more than the meditation, and driving back to Beverly Hills, he felt better, reflecting on what a primitive thing a man is, that a bellyful of good food could color the whole world differently. When he entered the police station, Beckman was waiting for him.

"Bingo," Beckman said to him. "Do you want to hear about it?"

"In a few minutes. First, where's Wainwright?"

"In his office. I got something for both of you to hear."

In Wainwright's office Masuto closed the door and faced Beckman and Wainwright.

"You're getting them tonight—all of them," Wainwright growled. "And so help me, Masao, you'd better come through!"

"Ah, so," Masuto said. "Would the honorable captain listen and stop shouting at me?"

"Not if you give me that shogun crap."

"I am trying to inject a note of lightness into a very miserable affair. I have been to All Saints Hospital, and I have been lectured to by our Dr. Baxter. It would appear that the Angel was a heroin addict. The glass of whisky that was handed to her when she returned was laced with chloral hydrate—"

"A Mickey," Beckman said.

"Exactly. And when she passed out, someone came into her room and shot her full of heroin."

"That would do it," Beckman agreed.

"More to come. The Angel was a man."

When Masuto had finished giving them every detail of Baxter's story, they still were unwilling to accept the facts.

"I just don't buy it," Wainwright said. "You can't turn a man into a woman—yeah, maybe into some kind of freak, but the Angel was no freak. She was one of the most beautiful dames I ever saw. She's been photographed and interviewed."

"She was stacked," Beckman said. "Those weren't falsies. Hell, that dressing gown didn't half cover her. She was all woman and built like something out of a *Playboy* centerfold."

"And she started out as a man. We may hate Baxter, but he's no fool. I saw the autopsy. So let's not waste time arguing about it. Now we know what she held over Mike Barton and what she blackmailed him with. As he saw it, if word got out that he had married a man, and that's the way they would have put it, he was done, finished as a star."

"No question about that," Beckman said.

"Perhaps, perhaps not. But that's the way he saw it."

"Didn't he know? I mean, when he married her?"

"Would you know?"

"You mean they could have slept together?" Wainwright asked.

"So Baxter tells me."

"I'll be damned."

"Do you think they knew?" Beckman asked. "I mean, the others."

"Maybe. If they did, they all lied. But maybe they didn't know—except—"

"Except who?"

"Kelly," Masuto said. "Well, we'll see. You said they're all coming?"

"That's right."

"Sy and I will get there by eight-thirty. We still have a few things to do."

Back in his own office Masuto said to Beckman, "All right, Sy, let's have it."

Beckman was still bemused. "What was she, a man or a woman?"

"Baxter calls it sexual reassignment. It's a long, complicated operative and hormonal procedure, and he says it's been done thousands of times."

"But how could Barton—"

"Come on, Sy. How could you? How could everyone else?"

"You tell me. It gives me the creeps. Was she an addict?"

"Yes."

"Heroin?"

"Yes."

"You know, Masao," Beckman said, "if anyone else was working with you, and you say to him, go out and search, he might just ask you what he was searching for."

"All right, you found it," Masuto said, looking at his watch.

"Well, why the hell didn't you tell me what I was looking for?"

"Because I didn't know what you were looking for."

"And now you know?"

"That's right."

"You are one weird son of a bitch, Masao. All right. I turned that place upside down. I found these in a jar of cold cream." He took three small ampules, each covered with a stretched rubber top, out of his pocket and placed them on Masuto's desk. "You know what they are?"

"Heroin?"

"Prepared stuff. I had Sweeney run a test. High grade, pure heroin, medicinally prepared, according to Sweeney, and legally imported from England."

"Illegal. I don't think a doctor can prescribe it in California, but I suppose that if you pay enough, you can get it. Well, that's what killed her, that and the whisky and the chloral hydrate."

"Where's the fourth ampule?"

"In the garbage at the Barton place, I imagine, or in a garbage dump somewhere. It wouldn't help us. Everyone's too smart about fingerprints these days. That was good work, Sy, damn good. Now what about the war records?"

"I unloaded that one on Keller. You were very nice to him, so he was very glad that we don't hate the FBI the way the L.A. cops and the New York cops do. I explained that we were a very small outfit and that we appreciated what the FBI could do for us. He said he'd call in the information as soon as Washington worked it up."

"Today?"

"That's what he said, this afternoon."

Masuto looked at his watch again. It was twenty minutes to three. "How long to get to the bank from here?"

"Our bank? Five minutes."

Masuto dialed the number of the Barton house. Elaine Newman answered, and Masuto said to her, "About that suitcase of money—did you see it open? Did you see the money?"

"Yes."

"Can you remember the bills on top? Tens, twenties, fifties?"

"They were twenties. I think—no, I'm pretty sure. I heard them talk about it after Mike left. Twenties."

Masuto did some quick calculations, and then he said to Beckman, "Sy, Polly has a draft for a thousand dollars waiting for us at the desk. Take it to the bank and get fifty twenty-dollar bills. Then stop at a stationery supply place and get ten reams of twenty-pound bond paper."

"How do I pay for the paper?"

"Tell them to bill us. Better hurry."

After Beckman left, Masuto sat at his desk, his eyes half-closed, his hands folded in his lap, and began to put the pieces together. He assembled them in his mind and let them fall into place, like the bits and pieces of a jigsaw puzzle. He was sitting like that when a cop opened his door and told him that Wainwright wanted to see him.

The city manager was in Wainwright's office, and he offered Masuto a bleak nod. "The captain's been telling me about tonight, Sergeant, and I don't like it. I think you ought to call it off."

"Why, if I may ask?"

"Because you're playing with fire. Jack McCarthy is one of the most important lawyers in Los Angeles, and a resident of this town to boot. Joe Goldberg is one of the biggest producers in town, and Ranier is a damned important businessman. And Hennesy—Sergeant, he's a member of the House of Representatives. You have money there and you have power, and sure as hell they'll slap us with a lawsuit that'll curl our hair."

"On what grounds? No one's being forced. No one's being charged. They're coming because they wouldn't miss tonight for the world. They're coming to see a killer exposed. I promise you that they will not be badgered or provoked. In fact, I won't even question them."

"Then what the devil do you want them for?"

"Because one of them murdered Joe Kelly, and because that man is an accessory to the murder of Mike Barton."

"Sergeant, I have a lot of respect for you, and I know what your record is. But how do you know that?"

"What I know is meaningless and unimportant until I can prove it, and unless you let this take place tonight, I doubt that I'll ever be able to prove it."

"Captain Wainwright tells me you're convinced that Angel killed Mike Barton."

"I am, yes."

"Can you prove it?"

"Possibly. Tonight."

"And who killed Angel?"

"I think I know, but I have no evidence, none whatsoever."

"I'd still like to know."

Masuto shook his head. "Then it would be an empty accusation. I don't do that. But about tonight, I can assure you that there'll be no heavy-handed police methods. I think you should allow it to proceed."

The city manager looked at Wainwright. "Captain?"

"I'll be there," Wainwright said, "so you can have my word that whatever is done will be done with a light touch."

"All right. But I'm holding you responsible. This kind of thing, three murders in one household, does the city no good. The sooner it's cleaned up and forgotten, the better off we'll all be."

Masuto's phone was ringing as he entered his office. It was Frank Keller, the very young FBI man, obviously pleased with himself. "I got it all, Sergeant," he told Masuto. "Shall I send the records over?"

"Can you give me the salient points over the phone?"

"Can do. Start with Joseph Goldberg. World War Two. Enlisted in 1942. Field artillery. Do you want the unit and battle record?"

"No. What about marksmanship citations?"

"Goldberg ended up a lieutenant, field commission. Small arms—that's common in the field artillery. McCarthy was World War Two as well, tank driver—can you imagine, with that paunch of his? Also small arms. Ranier was in the Korean War, quartermaster corps, no citations, and also in the Korean War, Hennesy served with the Coast Guard, rank of midshipman. That's it, very briefly. Should I send the records over?"

"I would appreciate that," Masuto said. "And thank you for your efforts."

Beckman came in while Masuto was speaking. "Anything?" he asked.

"Not much. They all know how to use a pistol."

"The paper's in my car. Ten reams—do you know what that weighs?"

"About the same as a million dollars in twenty-dollar bills, more or less."

"And the money's here," patting his bulging pockets. "It's a nice feeling to walk around with a thousand dollars in your pockets."

"Do you know where there's a paper cutter—one of those power jobs?"

"We could try City Hall. They should have one. I get the drift of what you're going to try, but what about the suitcase?"

"Courtesy of Gucci."

"Same one?"

"So Miss Newman says. I promised to return it, so we'll handle it carefully. Now let's try for the paper cutter."

Beckman took a packet of currency wrappers out of his pocket. "You forgot about these."

"So I did. I wonder what else I've forgotten."

12

The Suitcase

It was well after six o'clock before Masuto and Beckman finished cutting the paper and arranging the piles, topped by twenty-dollar bills, in the suitcase. While they were at work, Wainwright stopped by and watched them for a moment or two, and then said, "It's an old trick. What makes you think it will work?"

Masuto shrugged. "It's a shortcut. Maybe it won't work."

"You got anything else?"

"Something, not much."

"Whoever it is, he was in it with Angel."

"Yes."

"Then he could have killed Mike Barton."

"He could have, but I don't think he did," Masuto said.

"He could have killed Angel. One less to split."

Masuto shrugged.

"What does that mean?"

"I don't think he killed Angel. I think he killed Kelly."

"And what do we do about Angel?"

Masuto shook his head.

"You know," Wainwright said, "you are one secretive bastard, Masao. You're supposed to be part of this police force, not a goddamn supercop."

"I never think of myself as a supercop," Masuto replied, smiling. "I crawl through mazes and I try to guess what goes on in the minds of poor tortured madmen. Do you want me to drag you in with me every time I get some crazy notion."

"All I want you to do is to level with me."

"I try."

"And just keep an eye on that suitcase. I want that thousand dollars back."

"Not to mention the suitcase," Beckman said, "which cost four hundred and twenty dollars at Gucci."

"Goddamnit!" Wainwright snarled. "Who paid for it? Did you charge it to us?"

"Gucci lent it to us, as a gesture of goodwill toward the Beverly Hills cops."

"Clowns," Wainwright muttered as he stalked out.

They ate at Cantor's on Fairfax Avenue. Beckman wanted tempura, but Masuto had eaten tempura for lunch and he had no great love for Los Angeles Japanese restaurants. He told Beckman that he had a craving for chicken and matzo-ball soup so they went to Cantor's. Masuto would not talk about the case. He dodged Beckman's question and talked about the TV version of *Shōgun*, the matzo balls at Cantor's, and the problem of inflation on a cop's salary. Then, as they were leaving, he said to Beckman, "Do you know where to break the connection so that a car can't start?"

"Nothing to it."

"All right. Tonight, after they arrive, if there's a key in the car, put it into your pocket, and if there's no key, break the connection. But I don't want the cars damaged, I just want none of them able to start."

"No sweat."

"And if anything happens, just let it play out. No rough stuff, no daring moves, no jumping anyone. Just watch me and play my game."

"What are you looking for?"

"Just being careful."

It was eight o'clock when they got to Mike Barton's house, and the only car in the parking space was Elaine Newman's Mustang. Dempsy, still on duty, came out to meet them.

"No one here yet?"

"Only Miss Newman. She's been here all afternoon. The cook and the maid—that's all."

"Good. Now, listen, Dempsy, if something happens tonight, no guns or rough stuff. If someone has a gun, no shooting if you can help it. Play it very cool."

"What do you expect, Sergeant?"

"I don't know. Maybe nothing."

Beckman carried the suitcase into the house. "You know, Masao," he said, "I never thought of money being heavy. This is heavy."

Elaine Newman had opened the door for them, saying, "Thank God you're here, Sergeant. This place is spooky. What have you got in there?"

"About nine and a half reams of bond paper and some twenty-dollar bills. Do you have a closet in the library where you can stow it until we need it?"

"Absolutely." She was alive this evening. She had broken out of the torpor of her grief. "Get him," she said eagerly. "Get him, please. Not only for Kelly, but for Mike too."

"What do you mean by that?"

"Angel killed Mike, didn't she? That's what you think?"

"How do you know I think that?"

"You sit in this library, and you can listen to half the house. It's these old-fashioned hot-air vents. I overheard you talking to the captain. You know she killed Mike, but if she was in it with someone else, then that makes him guilty too, doesn't it?"

"Perhaps. I don't decide matters of guilt or innocence." He looked at her thoughtfully, reflecting that she was not beautiful, not even very pretty, but there was intelligence in the face and the wide-set, dark blue eyes were unusually striking. You saw the eyes before you saw anything else, and a head of rich thick brown hair framed them very well. She was an odd contrast to the woman Mike Barton had married and, very likely, Masuto decided, a complete reaction.

"Then get the evidence," she said evenly.

"I'll do my best." He turned to Beckman. "Cover the door, Sy, and steer each one into the living room. I don't want them wandering around the house. Be gentle but firm."

"It's like a goddamn convocation of nobility."

"Our nobility, for what it's worth. Lend a hand, please," he said to Elaine.

"Most of them I can't stand to look at."

Masuto smiled. "Rise above it. Serve coffee. Ask for drink orders. Be a sort of hostess."

"Must I?"

"You're all we have. Where are the ladies?"

"In the kitchen."

Going to the kitchen, Masuto tried to remember when he had spoken to the captain about Angel being the killer. Had it been here in the house? Too much had happened in the past thirty hours. Things ran together. In the kitchen was the warm, homey smell of baking. Lena Jones was filling a tray with cups, saucers, and cake plates. Mrs. Holtz was slicing a loaf cake.

"It smells wonderful," Masuto said.

"Have a piece."

"I just finished dinner."

"Have a piece. It won't hurt you. I'll pour a cup of coffee."

He sat at the table and munched the cake. "You're right. It's absolutely delicious. Lena," he said to the black girl, "yesterday, when Mrs. Barton died, Dr. Haddam tells us that you brought a glass of ice and whisky upstairs and that Mrs. Barton drank it. Can you tell me exactly how that came about?"

She was frightened. She stared at Masuto without answering.

"She's just a child," Mrs. Holtz put in. "You know what it's been like in this house yesterday and today? I'll tell you what happened. Kelly came into the kitchen. Lena and me were here. He says to Lena, 'There's a glass of whisky on the bar. Bring it up to Mrs. Barton.' I tell him, 'Why don't you bring it up yourself?' Then he curses. I don't want to speak bad of the dead, but he had a foul mouth. Then he stamps out of the back door."

Masuto nodded.

"You like sugar in the coffee?"

"No, just black. Lena," he said to the maid, "don't be afraid. Just tell me what you did then."

She took a deep breath. "I go out then and get the glass."

"What kind of glass?"

She went to the closet and took out a tall highball glass. "Same as this."

"Can you remember how many ice cubes were in it?"

"Three, I guess."

"You're a very observant young woman. And how high was the glass filled?"

She touched the glass about three quarters of an inch from the top.

"The doctor," Masuto said, "guessed that it was Scotch whisky."

"That's what she drank."

"Scotch is not quite as dark as bourbon or rye. Would you guess that it was all whisky, no water."

"Yes, sir, that's what I thought."

"And what did you do then?"

"I brought it upstairs. Mr. McCarthy and the doctor was just outside the door, and I hear it slam as I come upstairs. Then she opens the door, sees me, and grabs the drink out of my hand. She was shaking. She just drains it down and then pushes the glass back at me and slams the door again."

After that Masuto sat in silence for a few minutes, finishing the cake and the coffee. Then he said to Lena, "Do you think you can serve our guests tonight?"

"Yes, sir."

"They'll be here soon. Miss Newman will help you. Most, I imagine, will want drinks. Some will have cake and coffee.

Then, at about a quarter after nine, I'll get up and speak to them. When that happens, I'd like you to leave and stay here in the kitchen with Mrs. Holtz."

The Goldbergs were the first to arrive. They came at ten minutes to nine, and looking at the fat little man with a fringe of white hair around his bald skull, and thinking of the field artillery officer who got a field commission, Masuto reflected on the callousness of time. Captain Wainwright arrived a few minutes later, and then after him, Congressman Hennesy, Mrs. Cooper, and then Bill Ranier. It was ten minutes after nine before Jack McCarthy got there, completing the group, and he said to Wainwright, "I'm here only because Joe Smith asked me to come. Otherwise, I'd have no part of this nonsense."

Wainwright thanked him for coming. Elaine Newman took orders for drinks. Lena Jones poured coffee, her hands shaking just a bit. Della Goldberg and Bill Ranier had coffee. The others had drinks. Beckman stood unobtrusively at the entrance to the room. Elaine Newman took a seat apart from the others, who had seated themselves on three large couches that made a conversation area in front of the grand piano.

At half past nine Wainwright rose and spread his hands for silence. "I don't want you to think of this as an inquisition," he said. "Nothing of the sort. We asked you to come here tonight to help us inject some clarity into our thinking about this case. It's a shocking case, and it does the city no good, and until it's cleared up, it will engender fear where there's no reason for fear. Our procedure tonight will be very simple. Detective Sergeant Masuto will outline some of the salient points of the case, and when he finishes, anyone who wishes to can comment. That's about it."

Masuto stood up, and out of the corner of his eye he saw Lena Jones slip out of the room. There were no doors to the living room, but Beckman was planted solidly in the archway that led to the hall. The four men and the two women seated in the horseshoe of couches watched Masuto expectantly. Wainwright and Miss Newman were behind him.

Netty Cooper was finishing her second drink. "I think this is very thrilling," she said. "Our brilliant Fu Manchu is going to expose a murderer."

"Netty, don't be an ass," Hennesy said.

"Since you're an asshole, what difference does it make?" she replied.

"Lovely, lovely," Della Goldberg said.

"Oh, shut up and fry your own fish. Or make her the killer. Do make her the killer."

Masuto waited.

"I think we all ought to shut up and get this over with," McCarthy said.

"Can we begin?" Masuto asked. Silence. "Very well. Yesterday, Mr. Ranier informed me that the kidnapping of Angel Barton was not a kidnapping but rather a scam to defraud the government of income taxes."

"That was confidential!" Ranier cried. "You have no right—"

"I have every right," Masuto said coldly. "You did not put it to me as confidential. You laid it out in an attempt to save your own hide."

Ranier's face tightened, but he said nothing.

"The plan, in brief, according to Mr. Ranier, included himself and Mr. and Mrs. Barton. According to Mr. Ranier, Mike Barton was in default to the government for half a million dollars in back taxes, to which extent he would benefit from the swindle."

"Not true!" Goldberg snapped. "We had the same accountant. Mike was in default only fifty thousand dollars, and he had bonds to back that up."

"I told Masuto what Mike told me," Ranier protested lamely.

"Then, gentlemen and ladies, if Mr. Barton was not in default, we must look for another reason for his participation in so stupid and unworkable a scheme. Perhaps I can enlighten you—I mean those of you who are not already aware of what I am going to say. The woman, Angel Barton, had undergone a process of what is called sexual reassignment, a process which through hormonal treatment and surgery turns a man into a woman. This was the secret with which she blackmailed and controlled Mike Barton for two years."

Masuto watched the faces. McCarthy's face was full of disbelief. Goldberg was untouched. He knew. Della Goldberg burst into tears. Netty Cooper shook her head in disbelief, and Hennesy sat with his mouth open. Ranier's face was unchanged, set tight. Masuto turned to look at Elaine Newman. She was staring at the floor.

"So the kidnapping now stands in a somewhat different light," Masuto said. "Mike Barton was blackmailed into it, as he was blackmailed into remaining with Angel Barton, as he was controlled and manipulated—"

"I pleaded with him," Della Goldberg burst out. "I begged him to let the world know and be damned. Joe offered him an unbreakable five-picture contract if he would divorce that devil, but he wouldn't. He said it would be the end of his life, the end of his career."

"The plan," Masuto said, "as Mr. Ranier laid it out to Mike Barton, was for Angel Barton to meet him at San Yisidro, take the money, drive to downtown Los Angeles, park her car, and take a taxi back here. Instead, she altered the plan—with or without Mr. Ranier's approval, we have yet to discover—and when she met her husband, she sat down next to him in his car, diverted him somehow, took her gun from her purse, and shot him."

"Without my knowledge or approval, if there's a shred of truth in what you're saying, which I doubt!" Ranier shouted, and then turning to McCarthy, "Jack, can he do this? Stand there and slander me?"

"If he's slandering you," McCarthy said coldly, "it's actionable. You're not required to say anything or even to remain here."

"I damn well intend to remain here while he's spouting this garbage!"

Without appearing to respond to the interruption, Masuto continued. "Then, her husband dead, Angel put the suitcase in her car, drove downtown, and then took a cab back here. When she arrived here, she told Mr. Ranier what had happened, and he asked her what she had done with the gun. To his horror, she had forgotten to dispose of it. She gave it to him and he probably hid it for the moment behind some books in the library."

"I won't even dignify this fantasy with a denial," Ranier said.

McCarthy rose, one finger hooked on his belt. "You, sir," he said to Masuto, "have concocted a story which points directly to a man who is a client of mine. You have offered not one shred of evidence. Indeed, if you had any such evidence, you would not have provoked this charade, and since you cannot arrest Mr. Ranier, you have chosen to slander him. Let me be precise. You accuse him of conniving with Angel Barton to steal a million dollars, a hundred thousand of which was his own money—"

"Or his clients' money," Goldberg snapped. "The man's a business manager."

"I'll thank you not to interrupt me, Joe. But to get back to Sergeant Masuto's actionable accusations. You charge that the money was placed in Angel's car. You say she drove downtown, left the car, and returned here by cab. But when she returned, she had no money, no suitcase—"

As McCarthy spoke, Masuto nodded slightly at Beckman, who left the room.

"—which makes the first hole in your incredible concoction. And if Mike was being blackmailed so readily—" He stopped in mid-sentence as Beckman entered the room carrying what was unquestionably a very heavy suitcase. He placed the Gucci bag on the floor in sight of the group and opened it. The sight of the open bag, filled with what were apparently neatly stacked bundles of twenty-dollar bills, drew a collective gasp from the audience, the response of people to a magician who takes a very large rabbit out of an empty hat. Masuto watched Ranier, whose tight, controlled face revealed nothing. The silence was drawn like a stretched rubber band, until

Netty Cooper said shrilly, "Is that the ransom? Good heavens, did you have it all this time?"

"I didn't have it," Masuto said.

Coldly and angrily, Ranier said to McCarthy, "I want you to witness the fact, Jack, that my home was entered and searched illegally. I had no knowledge of the fact that Angel had put the ransom money in my house. I only discovered it an hour before coming here, and I intended to take up the matter with Captain Wainwright."

"Did you have a warrant to search his house?" McCarthy asked Masuto.

"No."

"Then I'm afraid you're in for trouble, Sergeant."

"Possibly." He nodded slightly at Beckman, who closed the suitcase and latched it.

"No, sir. Not possibly, but indubitably. Your conduct of this charade has been both disgraceful and actionable. You have read too many mysteries, sir. What fiction allows, the law prohibits—"

Still Masuto watched Ranier.

"—and I am absolutely amazed, Captain Wainwright, that you could lend yourself to this. However, this is not the end of the matter, only the beginning."

"May I finish?" Masuto asked sharply.

"I see no reason why this slander should be continued," McCarthy said.

"Your client is free to leave," Wainwright said with annoyance. "He was not forced to come here."

McCarthy looked at Ranier, who rose but made no move to leave. "Let's hear the rest of what this turkey has to say," Ranier said bitterly. "We might as well get all of it."

"Joseph Kelly," Masuto said, "was, as you all know, Mr. Barton's chauffeur. He was a man with a long prison record. Barton gave him a chance and employed him. Last night he was murdered. He was murdered because, standing in the butler's pantry, he overheard the conversation between Angel

Barton and Mr. Ranier when she returned here after the kidnapping."

"Just hold on!" McCarthy interrupted. "You're digging your own grave, sir! You're accusing my client—"

"Let me finish!" Masuto said harshly. McCarthy paused. "I'm not making any accusations that can't be backed up. There were two women in this house last night, Lena Jones, the maid, and Mrs. Holtz, the housekeeper, and both of them were awakened by a loud gunshot. Miss Jones looked out of her window and saw Mr. Ranier leaving Kelly's quarters."

It came like a bombshell. Even Wainwright and Beckman had not been ready for this. Only Elaine Newman appeared not to be surprised, sitting relaxed, a tight smile on her lips. The others were staring at Ranier, who shouted, "That's a damned lie, Masuto! That's a concoction out of the whole cloth! You set out to frame me here tonight! Loud gunshot! You son of a bitch, you said yourself that the gun had a silencer and that no one heard anything!"

"Wrong, Mr. Ranier," Masuto said. "No one except Captain Wainwright here and Detective Beckman knew about the silencer. How did you know, sir? How did you know that Kelly was killed with a gun that had a silencer?"

"You told me."

"I did not."

Ranier looked about him, stared at the three policemen who were standing calmly, then reached into his jacket, drew a gun, and stepped clear of the couches, covering the three policemen, who did not move.

"Nobody moves," Ranier snapped. "Just put your hands up and keep them there."

Just the slightest nod on Masuto's part to Beckman and Wainwright. They put up their hands, as Masuto did.

"Bill, you're crazy!" McCarthy cried. "What in hell are you doing? Can't you see this is a frame? You're playing into their hands."

"You—Newman!" Ranier said. "Pick up that suitcase and set it down by my side."

"Of course," Elaine replied. "I'm delighted to be of assistance, Mr. Ranier." And with a show of strength amazing in a woman so slight, she lifted the suitcase, carried it over toward Ranier, and then deliberately stumbled so that the whole weight of the suitcase caught him in the side. As he doubled over, Masuto sprang, grasped the wrist that held the gun, pointing the gun down as it went off. An instant later Ranier was lifted off the ground in Beckman's bearhug while Masuto forced the gun from his grasp. Then Beckman cuffed him.

"You bitch!" he snarled at Elaine Newman. "You filthy, lousy bitch!"

The room was in chaos, the others crowding around, Dempsy running in with his gun drawn, Elaine Newman smiling calmly, and Wainwright telling Masuto, "Read him his rights—slowly, carefully, every word of it. His lawyer's listening, so I don't want any mistakes from here on in."

"I arrest you for the murder of Joseph Kelly," Masuto said. "This is an admonition of rights. You have the right to remain silent—"

The voices were stilled. They stood in silence, listening to Masuto recite the formula as if it were some kind of prayer. When he had finished, Wainwright said to Dempsy, "Take him down to the station and book him for murder one and put him in the cage."

"I'd like to talk to him," McCarthy said.

"Downtown. Not here."

"I'll see Judge Lacey tonight," McCarthy said to Ranier. "We'll get bail."

"I doubt it," Wainwright said.

"We'll see," McCarthy said, and started to leave.

"One moment," Masuto told him. "Detective Beckman here fixed all your cars so they wouldn't start—just in case Mr. Ranier made it to his car. Give him five minutes."

By ten-thirty the last of them had gone, leaving only the three policemen and Elaine Newman, who was in the library. She said she had bills to pay, odds and ends to clear up, and she wanted it all done with so that she could get away to San

Francisco for a few days, see her mother, and begin to forget what had happened here.

Wainwright was staring unhappily at the Gucci bag. "What did you say was the price of this suitcase?" he asked Masuto.

"Four hundred and twenty dollars."

"Well, it has a bullet hole in it, so unless you can work it out with the Gucci people, that's four hundred and twenty dollars out of your pay, Masao."

"What? You wouldn't do that?"

"Wouldn't I? After your performance here tonight? You miserable son of a bitch, with your wild-eyed guesses and Chinese insights. You had nothing when you came in here tonight, nothing, and you hornswoggled me into backing you up and putting my job on the line. If Ranier wasn't such a stupid slob, he would have laughed you right out of the force."

"Wise men don't murder."

"Bullshit on your goddamn philosophy." He held up the gun. "This is all we got. And if this isn't the gun that killed Kelly, we got nothing."

"I think it's the gun."

"You think so. God save me from what you think."

"Even if he should beat the murder charge, it's a good arrest. We have him for armed robbery, for using the gun to get the suitcase out of here, and the feds can bring a conspiracy to defraud Internal Revenue against him. Also, I suspect that when they go through his books, they'll find enough illegal use of funds to send him away for a while."

"Maybe."

"Why don't you wait until Ballistics tests the gun and matches it. Then you can let go at me."

"Resisting arrest," Beckman put in.

"I'm going home," Wainwright said. He gave the gun to Beckman. "Drop it off at the station." But at the door, he turned back and said to Masuto, "Who killed Angel?"

Masuto shrugged.

"Don't give me that goddamn inscrutable crap of yours. I asked you a question."

"I can't answer it."

"You mean you don't know? Was it Kelly?"

"No."

"You're lying to me, Masuto. What is it? You got something you're going to dazzle us with?"

"No."

"Every damn reporter and wire service and TV camera in southern California is going to be at the station tomorrow. What do we tell them?"

"Tell them we have promising leads."

"Do we?"

"No."

"You think Ranier killed her and you got nothing to back it up."

"I think the person who killed Angel Barton was sitting in this room tonight, and we haven't one shred of evidence to back up a charge, and I don't think we'll ever have any."

"I've never known a lack of hard evidence to stop you before."

"It stops me."

"You can tell the media that a finger of suspicion points to Kelly," Beckman said. "The poor bastard's dead and that takes us off the hook."

"I hate that kind of thing."

"Then keep the file open," Masuto said. "Something may turn up."

Wainwright left. Beckman put the gun in his pocket, stretched, and yawned. "What about this Gucci suitcase?" he asked Masuto.

"Bring it down to the station, Sy, and separate the real bills and put them in the safe. I'll go over and plead my case with Gucci tomorrow."

"Okay. You coming?"

"I'll have a word with the two women in the kitchen. They must be pretty frightened. You go ahead."

"See you tomorrow," Beckman said as he went out.

13
Evidence

Masuto went into the kitchen, where the two women were sitting at the kitchen table. They had not left the kitchen since Lena returned there and they sat at the table in a kind of rigid expectation.

"What was the shot we heard?" Mrs. Holtz asked Masuto. "We were afraid to go in there."

"Nothing. Mr. Ranier's gun went off, but no one was hurt." Except myself, he thought ruefully, to the tune of four hundred and twenty dollars.

"Mr. Ranier?"

"Yes. He was the one who killed Kelly. We arrested him."

"A man like that! In his position!" Mrs. Holtz shook her head.

"Did he kill Mr. Barton?" Lena asked tremulously.

"No. Mr. Barton's wife killed him."

"How terrible!"

"Yes."

"And what happened to her?" Mrs. Holtz asked.

"Someone killed her."

"Death, death—it's so terrible."

"It's over now," Masuto told them. "It's all over. You're absolutely safe here."

"Should we just stay here?"

"I think so. As I said, it's absolutely safe. You can go on charging whatever food and supplies you need, and according to what Mr. Goldberg told me, payment will come out of the estate—as will your wages. Mr. Goldberg thinks that the house and most of Mr. Barton's estate was left to Miss Newman, but there's a bequest of ten thousand dollars to each of you—again according to Mr. Goldberg, so that should be helpful."

"Ten thousand dollars?" Both women looked at him in amazement and disbelief. "I can't believe it," Mrs. Holtz said, and Lena said, "I never in all my life—I'm just a black woman. Why he leave me that money?"

"He was a generous man. He knew how it felt to be poor," Mrs. Holtz said.

"Miss Newman is still here," Masuto told them. "She's in the library. So don't be alarmed if you hear someone walking around. I'll be going now. As I said, there's no danger, nothing for you to worry about."

He left the kitchen then and went to the library. The only light there was a green-shaded desk lamp. Elaine Newman sat at the desk, writing. She glanced up as Masuto entered, her face quite lovely in the dimmed light.

"May I come in?" he asked.

"Please. I'm just trying to tie up some loose ends. Mike's mother and father are dead, but there are a few relatives in the East who must be notified. The funeral's tomorrow, and while Mr. Goldberg's taking care of that, he wants me to write something for him to read at a memorial meeting which will be held a week later. It's not easy."

"No, I suppose not—to write about someone you love. No, it wouldn't be easy."

"You're a very sympathetic man, Sergeant Masuto."

"For a cop."

"I didn't mean that."

"No, I'm sure you didn't. You're leaving tomorrow?"

"After the funeral. I must get away for a while, and my mother will fuss over me, and I guess I need that right now. I feel very bereft and alone in the world."

"That's understandable."

"Won't you sit down, please?"

Masuto dropped into a chair, facing her.

"How did you know it was Ranier?" she asked him.

"I knew it, but I had to confirm it. That silly trick with the bag did it."

"But how did you know it?"

"There was a hundred thousand dollars of his own money in the bag—or his clients' money. That would make no difference. It was money he had in his hands. He was taking no chances. He would kill before he ever let that money out of his hands."

"And the money's at his house?"

"We'll have a search warrant in the morning, and we'll pick it up."

"I still don't understand how you knew," she said.

"The first thing he asked Angel when she entered the house was whether she had dropped the money at his house."

"But you weren't here when she came back."

"But you were, Miss Newman, here in this library. So you heard Angel—you yourself mentioned how the air vents carry sound—and I imagine Kelly, who was in the pantry, heard it as well."

"Really?" She put down her pen and looked at Masuto with new interest. "But there's no way you could have known whether or not I was here in the library, since you were not in the house."

"Perhaps."

"And I suppose you're also guessing that Kelly was in the pantry and that he overheard from there. Do you think that is why he was shot?"

"Yes. Probably he tried to shake down Ranier for part of the million dollars."

"And Ranier killed him."

"Yes."

"You still haven't explained how you knew about Ranier."

"Ah, so." Masuto stared at her thoughtfully. "You told me," he said.

"What?"

"Yes, Miss Newman, yesterday in the living room, after Mike Barton was killed, you lashed out at Ranier. You said something to the effect of, 'Are you going to kill me too?' "

"Did I? Truly?" She appeared not at all disturbed.

"Yes, you did."

"Well—" Elaine sighed. "I was upset, distraught, and I had to lash out at someone. Bill was there. I never liked him, and I begged Mike to get rid of him. He was stealing Mike blind. But come now, Sergeant, you didn't build your whole case on what I blurted out in a fit of grief and anger?"

"No, I didn't. You're absolutely right. And I wasn't wholly certain until our little ploy with the suitcase worked. But on the other hand, Miss Newman, I never for a moment believed that you would have indulged in that outburst unless you knew something. You're not the type. You are very cool, very collected, very much in control of yourself. There was also no doubt in my mind that Angel Barton had killed her husband. Of course, I could have been wrong."

"I don't think you were wrong."

"I know you don't," Masuto said, "because you were here in the library, and you heard Ranier ask Angel whether she had taken care of Mike, and you heard Angel tell him that she had. Then, I suppose, Ranier asked her what she had done with the gun, and she said she had forgotten to get rid of it. Ranier must have been very angry, and he took the gun from her and dropped it behind a row of books in here—"

"And never noticed I was here?" Elaine smiled.

Masuto pointed to the door. "You see how it opens inward. You simply stepped behind the door. Very cool and quick-thinking. If Ranier had seen you, he would have killed you."

"How amazing!" Elaine looked at him and nodded. "What a remarkable man you are, Detective Masuto! I had always thought that policemen had no imagination, but you have a marvelous gift of fancy. Please go on. I can't wait until I hear what happened next."

"You must have brooded about it for a while. I'm sure you loved Mike Barton a great deal. You would have made him a good wife."

"You're damn right I would!" she said, almost harshly, and then she began to cry. "Forgive me, please." She wiped her eyes with a tissue. "I'm all right."

"Can I get you anything? A drink?"

"No, I'm all right."

Masuto watched her and nodded. "You, you would have made him a good wife. You would have mothered him, and you have the wit and intelligence he lacked."

"Stop it! I don't want to hear about that! If you wish to continue your fairy tale, then do so. Otherwise, please go."

"I'll continue, Miss Newman. I don't know where you got the chloral hydrate, but I can guess. I would say that Angel had it and you found it in her medicine cabinet when she was out, and deciding that she intended to use it against Mike, you appropriated it. How you must have hated her! Of course, you knew her secret. Well, you waited for the proper moment, and it came when you heard Kelly shouting for Lena to get the drink and take it up to Angel. You had the chloral hydrate. You stepped into the hall and dropped it into the glass of whisky. Kelly had meanwhile gone into the kitchen. Then you waited until the coast was clear, took the gun from its hiding place, slipped up to Angel's bedroom, and found her unconscious, the chloral hydrate having done its work. Apparently, you knew where she hid her syringe and heroin—I don't think anyone else could have known that—and you gave her a large dose of heroin. I don't know why you took the ampule with you, possibly you were startled by some sound. You would have used the gun if you had to, but there was no need. You put the gun in her dressing-table drawer and you left. I suppose you flushed the ampule down a toilet. Yes, you must have hated her a great deal."

Elaine was herself again, and she smiled with approval. "What a stunning pattern of events you've invented. And you make it all fit together as neatly as a jigsaw puzzle. You're right about one thing, Sergeant. I hated Angel. Of course I knew about the sex change, but since it was Mike's secret in life, I was determined that it should be his secret in death. His Angel was a devil in human form, and I shed no tears for her. I'm glad she's dead. But tell me, do you actually believe this fairy tale you've put together?"

"I'm afraid I do."

"Are you going to arrest me for the murder of Angel Barton?"

"Only if you are willing to make a confession and sign it."

"And wouldn't I be a fool to do that, Sergeant Masuto? You haven't one tiny shred of proof or evidence to back up this complex story of yours. Not even enough to arrest me."

"I know that."

"And if you did, Mr. McCarthy, who was Mike's lawyer too, would be so happy to slap the City of Beverly Hills with an enormous false-arrest suit, not to mention defamation of character and mental stress."

"I know that too."

"I worshipped Mike. I adored him. He was my lover and my child at one and the same time. Bill Ranier was as guilty as Angel of Mike's murder. She pulled the trigger, but he was an accessory before the fact and after the fact. And I'll tell you something, Mr. Detective, in three years he'll be out of jail. You lied about Lena Jones. She's no witness. So what will they get Ranier for? Conspiracy to defraud the government? Resisting arrest? You said it yourself. He'll be out in three years or less."

"Possibly," Masuto agreed. "Unless you testified against him."

"You do so want life to fit your fantasies. But, you see, I wasn't in the library and I did not kill Angel, and I'm afraid we must leave it there."

Masuto stood up. "I don't believe in revenge, Miss Newman. The person who takes the revenge pays too great a price."

"But justice? Do you believe in justice, Detective Masuto?"

"I'm not sure that any of us are wise enough for justice. I'm not sure I know what justice is."

Elaine walked with him to the door. "I wish I could know you better, Mr. Detective. You're a very strange and interesting man."

"We never truly know another person," Masuto said. "Even Angel Barton had a spark of something human and wonderful buried inside her. Perhaps no one ever tried to find it."

"Whatever you think I've done," Elaine Newman said, "you're not making it any harder for me to live with it. I knew Angel Barton. You did not."

She stood at the door, watching him as he walked out and over to where his car was parked.